HOPE LARGE PRINT

AMISH ROMANCE

RUTH HARTZLER

ROMANCE BOOKS

Hope Large Print
Amish Romance
(The Amish Buggy Horse, Book 2)
Ruth Hartzler
Copyright © 2015 Ruth Hartzler
All Rights Reserved
ISBN 9781925689273

Scripture quotations are from The Holy Bible, English Standard Version® (ESV®), copyright © 2001 by Crossway, a publishing ministry of Good News Publishers. Used by permission. All rights reserved.

This is a work of fiction. Any resemblance to any person, living or dead, is purely coincidental. The personal names

GLOSSARY

Pennsylvania Dutch is a dialect, not a language, because it has no standard written form. It is written as it sounds, which is why you will see the same word written several different ways. All are permissible.

The word 'Dutch' has nothing to do with Holland, but rather is likely a corruption of the German word 'Deitsch' or 'Deutsch'.

Glossary

ab im kopp - addled in the head

Ach! (also, *Ack!*) - Oh!

aenti - aunt

appeditlich - delicious

Ausbund - Amish hymn book

bedauerlich - sad

bloobier - blueberry

boppli - baby

bopplin - babies

bro - bread

bruder(s) - brother(s)

bu - boy

Budget, The - weekly newspaper for Amish and Mennonite communities. Based on Sugarcreek, Ohio, and has 2 versions, Local and National.

buwe - boys

daag - day

Daed, Datt, Dat (vocative) - Dad

Diary, The - Lancaster County based Amish newspaper. Focus is on Old Order Amish.

Dawdi (also, *Daadi*) (vocative) - Grandfather

dawdi haus (also, *daadi haus, grossdawdi haus*) - grandfather's or grandparents' house (often a small house behind the main house)

de Bo - boyfriend

Die Botschaft - Amish weekly newspaper. Based in PA but its focus is nation-wide.

demut - humility

denki (or *danki*) - thank you

Der Herr - The Lord

dochder - daughter

dokter - doctor

doplich - clumsy

dumm - dumb

dummkopf - idiot, dummy

Dutch Blitz - Amish card game

English (or *Englisch*) (adjective) - A non-Amish person

Englischer (noun) - A non-Amish person

familye - family

ferhoodled - foolish, crazy

fraa - wife, woman

froh - happy

freind - friend

freinden - friends

gegisch - silly

geh - go

gern gheschen (also, gern *gschehne*) - you're welcome

Gott (also, *Gotte*) - God

grank - sick, ill

grossboppli - grandbaby

grossdawdi (also, *dawdi, daadi haus, gross dawdi*) - grandfather, or, in some communities, great grandfather

grosskinskind - great-grandchild

grosskinskinner - great-grandchildren

grossmammi (or *grossmudder*) - grandmother

gross-sohn - grandson

grossvadder - grandfather (see also *grossdawdi*)

gude mariye - good morning

guten nacht (also, *gut nacht*) - good night

gude nochmiddaag - good afternoon

gut - good

haus - house

Herr - Mr.

Hiya - Hi

hochmut - pride

Hullo (also, *Hallo*) - Hello

hungerich - hungry

Ich liebe dich - I love you

jah (also *ya*) - yes

kaffi (also, *kaffee*) - coffee

kapp - prayer covering worn by women

kichli - cookie

kichlin - cookies

kinn (also, *kind*) - child

kinner - children

kinskinner - Grandchildren

Kumme (or *Kumm*) - Come

lieb - love, sweetheart

liewe - a term of endearment, dear, love

liede - song

maid (also, *maed*) - girls

maidel (also, *maedel*) - girl

Mamm (also, *Mammi*) - Mother, Mom

Mammi - Grandmother

mann - man

mariye-esse - breakfast

mei - my

meidung - shunning

mei lieb - my love

mein liewe - my dear, my love

menner - men

mudder - mother

naerfich - nervous

naut (also, *nacht*) - night

nee (also *nein*) - no

nix - nothing

nohma - name

onkel - uncle

Ordnung - "Order", the unwritten Amish set of rules, different in each community

piffle (also, *piddle*) - to waste time or kill time

Plain - referring to the Amish way of life

rett (also, *redd*) - to put (items) away or to clean up.

rootsh (also, *ruch*) - not being able to sit still.

rumspringa (also, *rumschpringe*) - Running

around years - when Amish youth (usually around the age of sixteen) leave the community for time and can be English, and decide whether to commit to the Amish way of life and be baptized.

schatzi - honey

schee - pretty, handsome

schecklich - scary

schmaert - smart

schtupp - family room

schweschder - sister

schweschdern - sisters

schwoger - brother-in-law

seltsam - strange, unnatural

sohn - son

vadder - father

verboten - forbidden

Vorsinger - Song leader

was its let - what is the matter?

wie gehts - how are you?

wilkum (also, *wilkom*) - welcome

wunderbar (also, *wunderbaar*) - wonderful

yer - you

yourself - yourself

youngie (also, *young)* - the youth

yung - young

CHAPTER 1

Melissa fidgeted with her bonnet. It was all quite a shock.

"And so," Melissa's boss, Harriet Blackwell, continued, "you can see why I have to leave you in charge of the difficult clients. There's just no time to look for someone to replace me, and I don't know how long I'll be away."

"I don't feel confident speaking with clients," Melissa said. "Ever since I started working here at the *Marriage Minded Agency*, all I have done is filing. I haven't met a single client."

Harriet waved her concerns aside. "Nonsense. We don't have many difficult clients, and Milly will do all the other face-to-face work. The clients will be more respectful of you because you're Amish. They won't give you a hard time. You will simply have to watch what you say. Please try not to be as forthright as you usually are."

Melissa sighed. "I'll do my best." She knew there was no use arguing with Harriet, and besides, with Harriet's son suffering a badly broken leg in a motorcycle accident in Barcelona, and Harriet having to leave so suddenly, it would be selfish of her not to help out.

"Why can't Milly handle the difficult clients?" Melissa knew that Harriet's mind made was made up, but it was worth one more try.

Harriet frowned and crossed her arms over her chest. "Melissa, Milly handles all the face-to-face work with the clients, and she's overwhelmed as it is. More to the point, if a client progresses to the place where they need more input, they need to see someone different, and it's always been me. Now it will have to be you, at least until I get back."

Melissa nodded. *I don't have any choice*, she thought, *but perhaps it won't be as hard as I think.*

"And Melissa," Harriet continued, "can you work five days a week while I'm away?"

Melissa thought for a moment. "Sure, I suppose that will be okay with my mother."

Harriet shoved some papers into her briefcase. "Great, I'm so thankful, Melissa. Now I've got to run. Take the rest of the day off, but be here for an early start tomorrow. I'll call you when I get to Barcelona." She hesitated. "Well, I'll call you tomorrow some time. You'll be fine." With that, Harriet snatched up her briefcase and rushed out the door.

Melissa sighed. She thought of the Scripture, Proverbs chapter twenty seven, verse one - *Do not boast about tomorrow, for you do not know what a day may bring.*

That's for sure, Melissa thought. *I never really thought about that verse before. I do hope this is all in Gott's plan. I had no time to pray and think before agreeing to what Harriet wanted. All I can do is hope.*

The afternoon off was a small consolation to the thought of working five days a week and dealing with the agency's difficult clients, but at least the afternoon off would give Melissa a chance to catch up with her *gut* friend, Isabel.

Melissa hurried the few blocks to where Isobel worked, hoping to catch her in time for lunch. The Old Candle Store was always dimly lit, a fact Melissa always found amusing. After all, one would expect that a candle store would be bright. The brick walls and small, front windows added to the atmosphere, and the fragrance was delightfully overwhelming. Aged, wooden tables were crammed with every manner of candle, as were the old, wooden dressers which lined the walls.

Isabel looked up from behind the counter. "Melissa!" she exclaimed. "What are you doing here? It's not our day for lunch."

"Do you have time for lunch today? I've lots to tell you."

Isabel scrunched up her face. "Oh, that sounds exciting. I was about to go to lunch soon. I'll just ask my boss if I can go now. Won't be a minute."

Isabel disappeared into the back room, and soon returned. "*Jah*, Mr. Harrison says I can go right now."

The two friends walked to the nearby café where they met for lunch once a week. Unlike the candle store, the café had bright lighting and was modern, all sleek and sophisticated.

The girls sat at their usual table, which was right by the floor to ceiling glass windows overlooking the street.

"What's all this about?" Isabel asked as soon as they sat down.

"We had better order first, and then I'll tell you everything. You know how they don't like to wait for anyone to decide."

Isabel chuckled, and nodded at the waitress who was already making her way over. "I'm going to have the same as I always have," she said to Melissa, and then to the waitress whose pen was already hovering over her notepad, "The smoked ham, cold sandwich on multi-grain, sunflower bread please, and a chai tea latte."

"And I'll have the smoked salmon bagel, and a sugar and spice latte, please."

When the waitress left, Isabel laughed. "We're

creatures of habit. Always ordering the same thing."

Melissa shrugged. "Well, we know it's good." Taking in her friend's impatient expression, Melissa hurried to tell her the whole morning's events, an explanation that lasted half way through their meal.

"Are you sure you'll be all right with the difficult clients?" Isabel asked through sips of her latte.

"*Nee, nee*, that's what I'm worried about. Milly and Harriet are always talking about the difficult clients, how they're never satisfied. The difficult clients all have deep issues but don't know it, and Harriet is always telling them straight."

"But you're good at setting people straight," Isabel said. "You're quite blunt and say what you think."

Melissa cringed. "That's just it. Everyone's

always telling me that I'm not tactful, yet I don't think I'll be able to say anything blunt to these *Englischers*."

"I'm sure you'll be fine," Isabel said, but her tone was not convincing in the slightest.

CHAPTER 2

The following morning, Melissa and Milly stood over by the Nespresso coffee machine in the tiny, office kitchen. "I'll have to order more coffee soon," Milly said, throwing an empty packet of Livanto capsules into the trash. "Hey, Melissa, you're a million miles away."

Melissa bit her lip. "I'm worried about the difficult clients."

"I would be too, if I were you." When Melissa raised her eyes, Milly laughed. "Sorry, but there's no point sugar coating it, as you'll find out soon enough what you've gotten yourself into." Milly chuckled to herself.

"I didn't volunteer, that's for sure! Harriet said I had to do it. I've always been happy just doing the filing," Melissa said, "especially after all the stories you've told me about some of the clients. Seriously, that's why I don't want to get married—ever."

Milly shrugged. "They're not all that bad. It's just that some of them... oh well, you'll see."

Melissa took a mouthful of coffee and looked at the clock on the side wall. It was nearly nine, almost time for her first appointment. She made her way to Harriet's office and turned on the computer. "I really don't want to do this," she said aloud to herself.

The notes on the computer screen in front of her told her that her first appointment was Brian Adams. He was thirty two years old and, according to the notes, the agency had sent him on many dates and he had found none of the women suitable in the slightest.

Milly had attached a note to the file stating that Brian Adams was one of the most difficult clients that the agency had ever had. The note stated that Brian Adams was unhappy with the agency and was looking to go elsewhere. Melissa had to keep him happy by finding the perfect woman for him, or at least, a woman close enough to perfect to keep him at the agency. Harriet did not like to lose a single client and took such matters personally.

While Melissa was pondering the pressure under which her boss had placed her, there was a knock on the office door. She looked up to see Milly, along with a man standing behind her. "Brian Adams is here to see you, Melissa."

"*Denki*." Melissa coughed to cover up the fact that, in her nervousness, she had just spoken in Pennsylvania Dutch. No one else at the agency was Amish, so they would have no idea what she was saying. She amended her words to, "Thank you, Milly."

Melissa stood up and smiled at Brian. "Hello, Brian. Take a seat, please."

Brian sat heavily in the chair in front of Melissa's desk.

"Mrs. Blackwell has been called away on a family emergency. I hope you don't mind me helping you while she's away."

Brian's face contorted into a deep frown. "*Humph*, you couldn't do a worse job," he said rudely.

Melissa was taken aback by his attitude. "I see," she said slowly. "I've looked at your file and see that we've sent you on quite a few dates. Can you tell me your problem with these ladies?"

Brian crossed one leg over the other and waved his hands in the air as he spoke. "It's like this, none of the women were up to my standard in the looks department."

Melissa had heard that *Englischers* focused heavily on looks, and working at the *Marriage Minded Agency* led her to believe that what she heard was entirely true. "Brian, if you don't mind me speaking candidly to you..."

"Go right ahead," he snapped.

"Looks don't last."

Brian breathed out heavily and avoided eye contact with Melissa. "I need to be attracted to a woman, or it just doesn't work for me. I know people age and all that, but it would be good if they had looks to start with. I'm only attracted to younger women, but the agency keeps sending me on dates with women my own age. You know?"

Melissa nodded her head. What else could she do? She was working in a matchmaking agency after all, and from what Milly always told her, most of the men were the same. They all wanted young, attractive women who looked as though they were models. However, Brian Adams was not attractive at all. Melissa fought the urge to tell him that he was older and unattractive, so why would an extremely attractive, younger woman find him appealing? It made no sense to her, but apparently it made sense to Brian Adams.

Melissa gritted her teeth, knowing she had to do her job. "I'm sorry we've been unable to match you successfully so far, but there are two new women on the books that I can match you with." Melissa pushed forward the two photographs for him to look at.

He uncrossed his legs and leaned forward. "Now that's what I'm talking about." He chuckled in a predatory way, which made Melissa feel quite sick to the stomach.

He pushed the photograph of the blonde

woman toward Melissa. "I'll start with that one. Can you arrange for us to meet soon?"

Melissa nodded and forced a smile. "Certainly. I'll arrange it and email you the details."

Brian Adams left the office with a smile on his face.

Melissa felt sorry for the woman he ended up with, as all he was interested was the outside of a person. She was grateful she belonged to a community where modesty and humility were valued.

Her next appointment had her unconsciously straightening in her chair, wondering if her cheeks were pink and whether she had any sugar around her mouth from the donuts she'd had with her morning coffee. He was a handsome man.

This client's name was Anthony Pollard and he was new to the area. The notes stated that

Anthony came from a large family. At first appearances, he was softly spoken and appeared to be a respectful type of person. There was just something about him that made Melissa's heart pound inside her chest. Maybe it was the way his dark eyes sparkled when they looked at her. Or, it could have been the little indentation in the bottom of his strong chin.

"I have to ask you some questions, to help me find out why the dates have been unsuitable for you."

"Ask away." Even his voice was dreamy.

"What do you look for in a woman's personality?"

"Humor, I'd say. I like someone who can laugh at themselves and not take life too seriously." A particularly charming smile crossed Anthony's face.

"And? What kind of traits?"

"The usual kind of thing that people want, I suppose - kind, polite, respectful."

"And you definitely wish to get married?" The *Marriage Minded Agency* only took on clients who were serious about getting married, and Harriet frequently checked that the clients were still in agreement.

"I'm ready to get married. I am looking for someone who wants to settle down."

"Why are you looking for a serious relationship at this point in your life? Why now?" Melissa knew that Harriet always asked that question.

"I'm ready to have children." He chuckled. "And I can't do that by myself. What about yourself?"

Melissa looked up in fright. "Me?"

"Are you married?"

Melissa frowned. "No, I'm not."

"You have a boyfriend?"

"I'm the one asking the questions." Melissa was pleased she had cleverly avoided his question. "Now, can you tell me why your last date with Kate didn't work out?"

Anthony nodded. "Yes, I didn't choose her; Mrs. Blackwell did. She said that Kate was age appropriate for me. I don't want someone my own age! Sure, I'm getting on, but how many children would a woman be able to have if she were my own age? And I want lots of kids. I want a whole baseball team." Anthony laughed at his own joke.

Melissa sat there with her jaw dropped open. *Not another one*, she thought.

CHAPTER 3

Melissa was beside herself. The day was going from bad to worse. She had no idea what to say to the clients. She knew Harriet was strict with the difficult clients, but she had no idea how to walk the fine line between telling them the truth and not hurting their feelings.

Her next client was Debbie Worth. Debbie was a small woman in height but large in width, and she had not stopped talking from the moment she sat in the chair opposite.

Melissa had to interrupt Debbie, otherwise their time would be up. "Debbie, how was the last date we sent you on?"

"We didn't get on at all. Firstly, he didn't have a regular job and he was a smoker, when I strictly asked for a non-smoker."

While Debbie continued to talk about her last date, Melissa scanned the information on the man with whom Debbie had been on the last date. He was down as a non-smoker and a financier with a large firm. Melissa was nearly going to point that out to Debbie, but figured that there was no point. She would just call the man later in the day and ask him to update some details. "Excuse me, Debbie, but we have quite a lot to get through."

"Oh, yes, sorry. Everyone says that I talk too much. Go ahead—ask me some questions. In fact, ask me any question you like, but not about my last date, because I just told you about that date. It was not very good. Having said that, it wasn't awful, but it was just that I don't think we were very well..."

Melissa cleared her throat as a hint for Debbie to hush. "Debbie, moving forward, do you still consider that the questionnaire you filled out when you first signed up to the agency still represents the type of man you want, or have you changed your likes and dislikes in some way?" *Phew, that was a mouthful. It's exhausting to speak so much. I don't know how Debbie does it all the time*, Melissa thought.

"No, the same. I just want the same type of man that I wrote on the questionnaire. I did like the very first man the agency sent me on a date with, but I don't think that he wanted to see me again. Can you check into that?"

Melissa nodded. "I'll check into it for you." Melissa realized she needed training in how to be tactful. She had no idea what to say to

Debbie. The notes informed her that the first man Debbie had gone on a date with had found her an 'insufferable bore' and they had nearly lost his custom over such a bad date. The agency had since fixed that particular man up with someone with whom he had gotten on very well, and he was finally happily engaged to that woman. Melissa wondered how two people could go on a date, and one like the other, and the other dislike the other so much.

"Have you got a date to send me on this Saturday night?"

"We have a very nice man to send you on a date with. His name is Oliver Randall and he's a dentist."

Debbie looked very happy when she heard that the man was a dentist. "I like the sound of him already."

"I hope he's to your liking when you meet him. Here's the address and time that's been arranged." Melissa handed her a slip of paper. "Will that time and place be suitable?"

"That will be fine," Debbie said when she examined the slip.

"Good, we'll send you a confirmation email for the date with all the details."

"I'm very excited. I've never dated a dentist before."

"You've got lovely teeth. I'm sure he'll be impressed by them."

"You think so?"

Melissa nodded and hoped that the dentist would find Debbie to his liking. It was true - she did have nice teeth.

Debbie left, and Melissa sat down with her head in her hands. It wasn't even lunch time, but she felt as if she had done a whole year's work just that morning.

"Are you all right, Melissa?"

Melissa looked up with a start. "Milly, I didn't hear you come in. No, I'm not coping with these clients at all. I just want to get back to filing."

Milly simply shrugged. "There's only one more difficult client, and then you can get back to the filing. It's not as bad as you think. After all, you don't have to deal with them every day. Harriet wanted you to meet all the difficult clients at once, so that's why it seems so bad."

Melissa pulled a face. "I suppose it wouldn't be so bad if they were spread out."

"Well, the next client is Victor Byler. He should be here any minute, so you'd better read the notes."

Melissa nodded. This time, the notes did not say much at all. They simply said that all the women Victor Byler had dated had said that he was nice and polite.

Melissa was pleased that the next client would be polite, so she had quite a shock when he pushed past Milly, burst through the door, and exclaimed, "You're Amish!" as if it was a dire accusation.

Melissa stood up. "Hello. My name is Melissa Glick, and you will be seeing me instead of Harriet Blackwell, as she's been called away." She used her most formal, businesslike tone. "Please have a seat." She gestured to the vibrant, red chair in front of the desk.

Victor Byler sat down. "But, you're Amish," he sputtered, narrowing his eyes to tiny slits.

"Is that problem for you, Mr. Byler?" Melissa asked, all at once hit with the realization that *Byler* was an Amish surname. Perhaps this person was related to the Amish, which would explain his rather strange reaction.

"Not at all," Victor Byler replied in a cool tone. "I was simply surprised to see an Amish girl working at a business, let alone a matchmaking agency of all things."

Melissa bristled. "I can assure you, Mr. Byler, that the *Marriage Minded Agency* is a most reputable agency. We're not a dating service, but a matchmaking agency interested only in clients who wish to get married."

Victor Byler waved one hand in the air. "No, no, I realize that, of course. I just didn't expect to see an Amish woman here, that's all. It's not as if it's a quilting store or a restaurant, or even a furniture store."

Melissa glared at him, not knowing whether or not she should be offended. There was an uncomfortable silence, which Melissa finally decided she should break. "Mr. Byler, I've read the notes, and the ladies all seemed happy with their dates. Can you tell me why you weren't?"

"No."

Melissa had not expected him to say 'No'. She had expected some sort of explanation. "No?" she repeated.

Victor Byler shook his head. "I mean, I just don't know why. They were all nice. It's just that they weren't my type."

Melissa rubbed her chin. She already knew that the other difficult clients had issues; that was plain to see. Yet what issues did Victor Byler have? The previous dates had said that he was nice, courteous, and gentlemanly. He had not yet asked Melissa for a younger woman or an attractive one, but it was clear that he must have issues. She would just have it find out what they were.

"What *is* your type, Mr. Byler?"

A look of fear passed across Victor Byler's face. "I don't really know." Melissa raised her eyebrows, but he pressed on. "Well, someone who wants to have a family, who has old fashioned values, family values, and is a Christian."

"A Christian?" Melissa must have missed that in the notes, as she had not had time to read the whole file. She looked up to see Mr. Byler regarding her with narrowed eyes. "And the ladies you dated weren't Christians, and didn't have those values?"

Victor Byler shifted in his seat. It was clear he was uncomfortable. "No, not really."

"I'm so sorry, Mr. Byler. I'll be sure to find you ladies who are Christians and do have those values," Melissa said, again in her businesslike tone. "I'll be in touch when I've had a good chance to look through the files."

Victor Byler thanked her politely, and she showed him out.

Melissa went back to sit at Harriet's desk and put her head in her hands. "Oh that was awful," she said aloud to herself, "but at least that's the last of the difficult clients for the day."

She let out a long sigh. Victor Byler didn't seem so difficult, at least not as difficult as the others. In fact, he was tall and indeed handsome, with his broad shoulders and bulging biceps, and she had never seen eyes like his before, a deep hazel with golden flecks through them. *From what he said, I'm his ideal woman*, she thought with some amusement, *or at least the English version of me would be, if there was one*. Melissa chuckled.

Victor Byler walked only a few steps down the corridor and then leaned against the wall. *An Amish woman!* He had done his best to avoid the Amish, and had no idea he'd find one at the *Marriage Minded Agency* of all places. Cold beads of sweat broke out on his forehead and he hastily wiped them away.

He was fine speaking with the bishop, but he was not comfortable having any dealings with any other Amish person, especially not an Amish woman, and especially not an attractive Amish woman with blue-green eyes and a pretty face.

CHAPTER 4

Melissa helped her *mudder* carry the *schnitz und knepp* to the table. It was Melissa's favorite dish, and, while it took some time to prepare, the actual baking was rather easy. She loved the flavor of the apple with the ham, as well as the contrast of the sweetness of the brown sugar with the tartness of the apples.

After they shut their eyes for the silent prayer, Melissa was the first to speak. "It feels so quiet here now, without Daniel and Nettie living here."

Mrs. Glick looked sad. "*Jah*, we miss them, but it was nice that they stayed here as long as they did after they were married. If they hadn't had Nettie's *haus* to move into, they would have stayed longer."

Melissa nodded, and ate a mouthful of food.

"Still," Mrs. Glick continued, "I'm sure there will be lots of little *bopplin* soon."

"I hope you mean Nettie's *bopplin*, *Mamm*, as I don't intend to get married until it's almost too late for me to have *bopplin*. I've had quite enough of *menner*." Melissa noticed that her parents exchanged glances.

"Is it your work at the matchmaking agency making you feel that way?" her *mudder* asked.

Melissa nodded. "*Jah*, and *Mamm*, I completely forgot to tell you. My boss, Harriet Blackwell, had to go to Barcelona suddenly, and she wants me to interview her most difficult clients, and that means that I'll have to work five days a week. Will that be all right with you? It's only temporary, until she gets back."

Mrs. Glick frowned, but said, "That will be fine, I suppose. Nettie is still working in the garden for me."

"It's just the horse," her *vadder* said.

"Oh sorry, *Daed*, I forgot that you would need the buggy."

Mr. Glick stroked his *baard*. "*Nee*, that will be all right too. Daniel and Melissa don't need two buggies and two buggy horses. I'll ask them if you can borrow one buggy and their palomino horse."

"Blessing?" Melissa's face lit up.

"*Jah*." Mr. Glick smiled. "Nettie always said that Blessing was a gift from *Gott*, as Blessing led her to Daniel. Perhaps Blessing will lead you to a *gut mann*."

"Matthew, don't be *ab im kopp*." Mrs. Glick scolded her husband in a lighthearted manner.

"I don't want a *mann*." Melissa sighed. "I met some irritating *menner* today."

"Not all *menner* are irritating," Mrs. Glick said, which drew a chuckle from her husband. "Anyway, Melissa, what did these *menner* do that was so irritating?"

Melissa sighed loudly. "They wanted young, attractive women, when they themselves were neither young nor attractive."

"*Englischers*," Mr. Glick said with a sigh. "Most of them look at the outside of the person. Remember what *Gott* said to Samuel, 'Do not look on his appearance or on the height of his stature, because I have rejected him. For the Lord sees not as man sees - man looks on the outward appearance, but the Lord looks on the heart.'"

"*Jah*, I know that, *Daed*," Melissa said, "but

the difficult clients don't. One client wanted a woman simply so she could have a lot of children for him. It was all I could do not to be forthright and tell him what I thought of that."

Her *vadder* looked amused. "That must have been difficult for you, indeed, as you usually have no problems saying exactly what's on your mind."

Melissa scrunched up her face, but had to agree that her *vadder's* words were correct. She was forestalled from responding by a knock at the door.

"*Hullo!*" Melissa at once recognized the voice as belonging to her *Aenti* Sylvia, her *mudder's schweschder*.

"Sylvia!" Mrs. Glick hurried to the door. "Come in, come in, and have some dinner. Melissa, fetch more *schnitz und knepp*."

When Melissa returned with the *schnitz und*

knepp, she saw that her *Aenti* Sylvia and her *Onkel* Amos had with them a young *mann*.

Sylvia smiled broadly when she saw Melissa. "Melissa, *wie gehts?*"

"I'm *gut*, thank you." Melissa eyed *Aenti* Sylvia warily. She was always trying to introduce her to young *menner*, and now she had actually gone so far as to bring one to the *haus*.

"Melissa, this young *mann* is Raymond Burkholder. He'll be staying with us for a while." She gave Melissa a big wink, much to Melissa's dismay.

No more was said until everyone was seated and happily eating their meal. "Raymond came from another community," *Onkel* Amos said. "The bishop asked if he could stay with us, as he's just taken up work here."

"What sort of work have you taken up here, Raymond?" Mr. Glick asked.

Raymond looked around the table, and

fidgeted nervously before answering. "My *familye* had to sell the farm, so I've come here to start an apprenticeship as a cabinet maker."

"*Gut, gut*," Mr. Glick said. "That is a *gut* trade to get into."

"*Jah*," Aenti Sylvia agreed, shooting Melissa a pointed look. "It won't be too long before he will be able to provide for a *fraa*."

Melissa at once was embarrassed, and noted Raymond was too, as their eyes met and then they both looked away. Nevertheless, Melissa did not blame her *aenti* for wanting to matchmake, as uncomfortable as it made her feel. It was difficult for a young woman who wished to marry, as there was a short supply of young *menner* and young women in the community. Suitable matches were made early, and it was rare that someone new came into the community. Her *aenti* only had her best interests at heart.

Melissa and her *mudder* rose to clear the plates

away, and soon returned to the table with shoo-fly pies. "Melissa made these the way she likes them," Mrs. Glick said, "wet bottom, without much crust."

Aenti Sylvia nodded her approval. "*Jah*, why dilute all that molasses and brown sugar with a thick layer of crumbs on the bottom. The layer of crumbs on top is enough." She patted her ample stomach and everyone laughed.

Mr. Glick turned once again to Raymond. "So, Raymond, are you working for Martins' Joinery, the Mennonite business downtown?"

Raymond once again appeared to be nervous to be in the spotlight, and wrung his hands. "*Nee*, I'm working for Classic Custom Cabinetry."

Mr. Glick nodded. "*Jah*, I've heard of them, very good workmanship, everyone says. They have a fine reputation."

Onkel Amos agreed. "Raymond was blessed to

be offered an apprenticeship. The bishop knows the owner and told Raymond's bishop."

Mr. Glick scratched his head and addressed Raymond once again. "The bishop knows the owner of Classic Custom Cabinetry? But it's not an Amish-run business."

Raymond had just taken a big mouthful of shoo-fly pie and pointed to his mouth to excuse himself for not answering at once. He swallowed rapidly and that made him cough. *Aenti* Harriet patted him hard on the back, which made his eyes stream. Melissa felt quite sorry for him.

"I believe the owner's *familye* was Amish, or the owner was once Amish, or something like that," Raymond managed to say between coughs. "Perhaps he went on *rumspringa* and became English. I'm not really sure of the details."

"But he has clearly kept in touch with the bishop," Mr. Glick said.

Raymond simply nodded as he reached for his glass of water.

"And they say women are the gossips and want to know everything," Mrs. Glick said to *Aenti* Harriet, and everyone laughed.

"I didn't know the owner of Classic Custom Cabinetry had any Amish connections either," *Onkel* Amos said, "not until Raymond told me. What's his name again, Raymond?"

"Victor Byler."

Melissa nearly choked on her Shoo-fly pie and went into a fit of coughing when some crumbs went down the wrong way. Thank goodness she was sitting opposite *Aenti* Harriet, as she did not wish to be slapped hard on the back.

Victor Byler? The difficult client? The one with the golden-flecked eyes and the polite manner?

It was possible Victor Byler had once been Amish?

CHAPTER 5

Melissa was happily driving Blessing to work.
No difficult clients were scheduled for face-to-
face appointments that day, and she was
relieved she would be able to spend the day
filing, as well as going over the difficult clients'
files.

She was also happy as her *bruder,* Daniel, had
delivered the palomino buggy horse, Blessing,
to her that morning, complete with Daniel's
wife's buggy. Blessing proved to be easy to
drive and very responsive, unlike her *familye's*

buggy horse, Tom, who was reliable but a bit of a plodder.

Melissa was enjoying the crisp morning, and was looking at the various shrubs and trees of laurels, hemlock, black birch, and white pine along the roadside. Soon she left the winding roads behind her, and came out onto the road which headed downtown. To her relief, Blessing was sturdy in traffic and did not react when cars skimmed too close to him.

Her thoughts turned to Victor Byler. Had he once been Amish, but had left his community after his *rumspringa*? That would explain his initial reaction to her. Or did he simply have Amish relatives? She could hardly ask him. After all, he had not volunteered the information and she had to be discreet. What would her boss, Harriet, do in that situation? Melissa chuckled to herself. Harriet would no doubt come straight out and ask him, but Melissa felt as though she could not.

As she approached the agency, a silver-gray car overtook her slowly. *A more considerate driver than most*, she thought, but then saw that the driver was leaning over, staring at Blessing. The driver looked like Victor Byler.

What's wrong with me? she asked herself. *I'm starting to imagine him now.* Melissa shook her head hard as if to erase all thoughts of the mysterious and attractive Mr. Byler.

When Melissa drove Blessing into the agency's parking place reserved for her buggy, there was a man leaning against the silver-gray car parked nearby, the same car that had overtaken her just down the road. She jumped out at once and tied Blessing to the rail.

"I thought it was you driving," Victor Byler said by way of greeting.

Melissa groaned inwardly. *I hope he's not here to complain*, she thought. *Couldn't he have come to the office? And I thought I'd have a day free of difficult clients.* She got down from the buggy and turned to face him, but to her surprise, Victor Byler walked straight past her and over to Blessing.

"I'm shocked! I'm shocked!" she overheard him mutter to himself.

Blessing nuzzled him happily and he stroked Blessing's face.

"Why, he's the image of my old horse, Dan. I can't believe the likeness. I almost thought I saw a flicker of recognition on his face when he saw me. It can't be! it can't be!"

"Perhaps he *is* your horse," Melissa said. "My *bruder* found him and could never find the owner."

Victor Byler finally turned to Melissa. "It can't be the same horse. Dan was my horse when I was just a boy. Your horse does look just like my Dan. Anyway, what's his name?"

"Blessing."

"Blessing," he repeated, looking thoughtful. "Would you mind if I bring Blessing carrots from time to time? I really miss my horse. I've missed horses since I moved here. I work only a couple blocks away."

"In the kitchen construction business?"

Victor Byler narrowed his eyes and pursed his lips. "Yes?" It came out as a question.

Melissa simply said, "Certainly you may give Blessing carrots. I'm sure he'd love that, and he loves attention too."

Victor Byler beamed at her. "*Denki*, Miss Glick." With that, he patted Blessing once more and then strode away.

Melissa stood watching him walk away, her mouth open. *Did he say 'Denki' because he knows that I'm Amish, or because he was once Amish and let the word slip?* Melissa stood there a while pondering the question, but finally rallied, telling herself that she would have no way of finding out unless she asked him, and she certainly had no plans to do that.

Victor Byler made his way back to his cabinetry store, but all thoughts of cabinetry were far from his mind. He called into the café he usually frequented, and absently ordered an espresso.

"You're late today, Mr. Byler," the cheerful barista greeted him.

Victor eyed the young man warily. "*Err*, yes," he said.

"Obviously overdue for your caffeine hit, are you?"

"*Err*, yes," he repeated, and then walked slowly out of the café.

Victor Byler was shaken by his encounter with the Amish woman and her horse. Was this

God's doing? Victor shrugged as he walked along. Who would know?

He had put the Amish behind him, but now it was as if he had no way of avoiding them. Why, even the horse was the image of his old horse, Dan. The girl made his heart flutter, but that was a dangerous path, and one he had no intention of taking. How had this happened to him? He would have to avoid the girl from now on.

Yet, despite his best intentions, Victor Byler found himself giving carrots to the palomino buggy horse, Blessing, right on five that afternoon, the very time he figured that the girl would leave her office.

However, there was no sign of her, and by ten past five, he was down to his last carrot. And so it was with a mixture of relief and misgivings that he heard the sound of Amish boots behind him. He turned around.

"Hello, Miss Glick."

"Hello, Mr. Byler."

Was she already betrothed to an Amish man? He could not ask, of course, and he rebuked himself for even wanting to know. She made his stomach churn and affected him in a way which no other woman ever had.

CHAPTER 6

Melissa raced into Milly's office. "Milly, I've just had a call from Barcelona from Harriet. She said that she's reviewed our client files, but then the phone crackled and cut out. I'm sure she said for me to go to dinner with Victor Byler. That wouldn't be right, would it?"

Milly laughed. "With all our difficult clients, one of us goes to dinner with them to see what their issues are."

"And that helps?" Melissa asked.

Milly raised her eyebrows. "Of course it does. Otherwise we wouldn't do it. They're more relaxed out of the office and tend to open up more. Since you've already had some contact with Victor Byler, it's best if you do it."

"Do what exactly?" Melissa had a feeling she wouldn't like the answer.

"Take him to dinner. The agency will pay, don't worry. All you have to do is get him talking about himself—well, his expectations mainly. When you get back from the dinner, then you type out a report for our file. From the file, we'll see if we can make any better matches for him."

Melissa immediately felt sick to the stomach. Going out to dinner with a man would be like a date. She'd never been on a date with a man and did not want her first dinner alone with a man in a nice restaurant to be with an *Englischer*.

And should she ask the bishop? To her it was

most unseemly thing to do. She hoped Victor Byler would not think that she was attracted to him in any way. There was only one thing for it, she would have to stay in control of the conversation from start to finish.

"Melissa, Melissa."

Melissa suddenly realized that Milly was been trying to gain her attention. "I'm sorry. I was lost in thought."

Milly shook her head and laughed. "Focus, Melissa, focus. This could be good training for you, if you want to move up in the company." Milly winked.

Melissa smiled. "Stop teasing me, Milly. You know I don't want to move up in the company." She was not sure if she was cut out for this type of business. Maybe she would be better off doing something where there was a little less contact with *Englischers,* particularly handsome ones like Victor Byler.

"It's all arranged for tomorrow night."

"The date?" Melissa's hands flew to her throat. "I mean, the dinner with Victor Byler?"

"Yes, the dinner with Victor Byler." Milly handed her the details on a slip of paper. "Be ten minutes early and have your notes ready. Read the file about him beforehand."

"I'm a little nervous, as I've never taken a client to dinner before." Melissa wanted to add that she hadn't been alone with a man at a restaurant before, but that would sound as if she had lived too sheltered a life. She decided to keep quiet about her lack of experience with *menner*. Sure, Milly knew she was Amish, but Milly did not have to know that she had never been interested in any *mann*.

"There's nothing to it," Milly continued, waving her hands in the air to emphasize her point. "Just have a polite conversation at first to get him in a relaxed mood, and then find out what he wants in a woman. You can also see if he's doing things that would put a woman off, such as bad table manners, belching loudly, and the like." Milly looked at Melissa, who was laughing at her words. "Don't you worry, that does happen!"

After she had finished speaking to Milly, Melissa rushed back to her desk, grateful that it was near the end of the day.

That night and the whole next day passed in a blur of nervousness as Melissa could think of nothing other than her date with Victor Byler. No, it wasn't a date, she had to remind herself constantly. It was just a dinner and it was purely for work. *A business dinner*, she said to herself yet again. If she was this nervous, she wondered how nervous she would be on her first real date with a *mann* whom she liked and who liked her back.

She pressed both hands to her nervous stomach. Surely she could do this. *It's part of the job*, she told herself.

The taxi left her at the restaurant door ten minutes early, as her boss had suggested. She was glad she would be able to have a few quiet moments to get her head together. As she walked through the door of the restaurant, a woman with a folder under her arm greeted her.

"Um, I'm Melissa Glick. I have a reservation booked for seven." To her dismay, her voice trailed upwards at the end. Melissa realized that she sounded absolutely childish and not confident in the slightest. She cleared her throat and straightened her back. The woman simply smiled and showed her to the table.

To Melissa's surprise, Victor was already at the table. He smiled widely and stood to his feet as she approached.

CHAPTER 7

Melissa could not take her eyes off him. She felt as though she were in a dream. Everything seemed to be going slowly—it was as if they were the only two in the room. His dark, good looks were accentuated by his crisp, white shirt, the same bright white as his straight, white teeth. He wore black pants, and Melissa wondered whether the *mann* she married would make her feel the way Victor was making her feel right now.

Breathe, Melissa, *breathe*, she told herself after

she realized she had been holding her breath. She let out her breath all at once, and it turned into a little gasp as she held out her hand for him to shake. "Mr. Byler, you're early."

They sat down.

"Please call me Victor," he said, and then continued before Melissa had a chance to respond. "I always like to be early, an annoying habit I picked up from my family."

Melissa nodded and wondered whether Victor Byler was aware just how nervous she was. It was all right for him. After all, he'd been out to dinner with women many times, and besides, this wasn't even a proper date. Melissa's heart pounded and her face flushed. She saw that there were already two glasses of water on the table. She reached for the glass. Maybe a large mouthful of water would soothe her nerves. Just as her hand was about to touch the glass, Victor said something which caused her to look at him, and then she knocked the glass over.

They both stood to their feet quickly as the water spilled over the table in all directions. Victor laughed.

"Oh, no. Look what I've done," Melissa said, as she looked down to see if water had spilled on her over-apron.

A waiter at once rushed toward them with a large white cloth.

Another waiter came up to their table and said, "We'll seat you at this table." The waiter pulled out the chairs at the table next to them.

After they sat at the other table, Melissa said, "I'm so sorry, Mr. Byler, um, I mean sorry, Victor."

Victor could scarcely keep the smile from his face. "Well, so far this has been the most eventful dinner I've ever had, and it's barely begun."

Melissa laughed and immediately relaxed. "Don't tell on me, will you. To the agency I mean."

Victor laughed some more. "I won't tell them that you're a bit of a klutz."

Melissa laughed. "I'm not a klutz. Well, not usually." Yes, not usually, unless she was sitting in front of a stunningly handsome man who made her heart race out of control.

After they had perused the menus and ordered their meals, Victor spoke. "So tell me, Melissa, what do you do in your free time?"

"I don't seem to have much free time. When I'm not working, I do a lot of chores for *Mamm* and *Daed*." Melissa realized she was again reverting to Pennsylvania Dutch. "I mean my mother and father." She was not going to be the one doing all the talking; she had to get him to speak about himself. "Tell me what *you* like to do in your spare time."

"I started a business a while ago and that keeps me busy. I try to lead a balanced life and not work all the time. I could very easily work seven days a week, but I learned a long time ago to prioritize things."

"How so?" Melissa asked, remembering the instructions she had given herself before she came—she had to keep control of the conversation.

"I know what I want out of life, and if I work from the time I wake up until the time I go to sleep, every day of the week, then that would just be no good at all. I'd grow my business a lot faster and make a lot more money, but I want more for my life than just money."

Melissa looked at his golden-flecked eyes. She could lose herself in them very quickly. When she realized she was staring into them a little too long, she came to her senses and asked, "What other things do you want?"

"I want a family. I want a happy household, the same as the household I was brought up in."

Melissa found herself glowing from within. *I like this mann. Maybe all Englischers aren't the same*, she thought. Her thoughts were interrupted by their meals arriving.

When Victor finished his first mouthful, he said, "Don't think you are leaving here tonight without telling me something of yourself. I don't care that this is a dinner to find out how you can better find a match for me. If I'm honest, I find you intriguing." Victor leaned toward her and said, "I'd like to know how an Amish girl finds herself working at a dating agency."

Melissa smiled and said, "That's a story for another time. This dinner is about you." *Gut girl, Melissa, keep control.* Melissa silently congratulated herself for her quick thinking.

Their small talk throughout the meal was pleasant, so pleasant, in fact, that the need to run suddenly came upon Melissa. She should get away from this man. She knew for a fact that she wasn't just attracted to his looks, in the same way that the shallow men at the agency were attracted to women. Sure, he was good looking, but it was his gentle nature and his kind ways that really made her heart beat faster. She had assessed him as a *mann* who was looking for an honest, sweet girl with good morals, who found pleasure in the simple things in life. Could it be that what Victor wanted was a girl just like her?

"I must go," Melissa said. Yes, go before she developed an even bigger attraction to this *English mann.*

"No, stay. I hear the desserts here are out of this world."

Part of her wanted to stay, but the sensible part of her knew that she must go, and go immediately. "No, I don't eat desserts," she quickly fibbed, and then hoped *Gott* would forgive her.

"Forget the desserts. Surely, you can stay and talk, just a few more moments?"

"I must go. I'm sorry." Melissa stood up, and Victor stood up as well.

Melissa walked to the cashier to pay with the company credit card.

"I'll pay for this, Melissa. I've had the best night I've had since I can't remember."

Melissa fought the urge to be flattered. "No, it's all arranged. The agency's paying as part of their arrangements with you."

"Why, it's Isaiah Byler!"

Both Melissa and Victor swung around at the loud voice far too close behind them. A short blonde man, around thirty years of age, stood looking directly at Victor.

"Levi, what are you doing around these parts?" Victor quickly spun back around to Melissa. "Thank you for that, and I'll see you another time." He put his hand on the stranger's shoulder and led him to the other side of the restaurant as they talked.

Melissa kept her eyes on them, without trying to be obvious, while they processed the credit card. It seemed Victor had forgotten all about paying.

"There you go, Miss." The lady handed her back the card.

Did that man call him Isaiah, before Victor hurried him away? So that means that his real name might be Isaiah Byler? An Amish name if ever I heard one. Melissa walked to the door and then glanced stealthily over her shoulder at Victor. It was clear that he was deliberately not looking at her, while he talked to the *mann*

73

whom he had addressed as *Levi*. However, despite the fact that Levi was not wearing Amish clothes, Levi was an Amish name. *What is Victor keeping from me?* Melissa wondered.

CHAPTER 8

"How was your dinner last night with Victor Byler?"

Melissa looked up as Milly bounced through the office door. "It was fine," she said, trying not to give too much away.

"Love, what a tricky thing," Milly said, waving one hand at Melissa. "Some people get it from the first, and some look for it their entire lives but never stumble over it. That's so cruel. Love can cause so much misery. Every day I hope I can make at least somebody happy. Do you believe in karma?"

Melissa raised her eyebrows. "No, I don't."

Milly giggled. "Well, I do. I know I deserve to be happy, after all the efforts I made for the clients. Surely all that altruism, all that good will, hasn't been for nothing!"

Melissa pursed her lips and stared at Milly. "Have you had too much coffee again?"

Milly sobered up immediately. "Yes, as a matter of fact. Boyfriend troubles."

Before Melissa could ask, Milly pressed on. "So, this morning, would you go through the files to find a suitable match for Victor Byler? I hope your dinner with him gave you some insight into his issues. He seems nice enough to me, and the dates have all liked him, but so far he hasn't found anyone suitable, no matter what kind of women we've sent him on a date with. There must have been always something about them that he didn't like, although he would never tell us what it was. Is he looking for perfection?"

Melissa was about to respond, but Milly kept talking. "I just wish the difficult clients would get the fact that there's no such thing as perfection. The power of love makes us forget about all about someone's minor defects and differences. Love should make us happy, but some people seem to self sabotage. Perhaps he's one of those."

"Perhaps." Melissa was glad she managed to get a word in. "I'll get myself some coffee, but I don't think you should have another one." Milly laughed and flounced out of the room.

Melissa was not looking forward to finding a date for Victor right away, so she made herself some coffee, and stretched her bones for a little bit, before she looked at the file on his dating history. She had skimmed it previously, but now looked at it with renewed interest.

Looking at page after page of dating failures, Melissa felt quite sorry for him. All the dates had spoken highly of him and stated that they wanted another date. There were no exceptions. So what was Victor's difficulty? How had he found so many problems with each woman that he did not want a second dinner date?

Melissa looked through the new clients for a match. There was a lady called Linda who said she had Christian values and wanted a family. The others had actually said that too, but at least Linda was new to the agency. After two cups of coffee, Melissa could not find anyone more suitable than Linda, so she decided that Linda would be the one she would send to dinner with Victor.

Melissa sat back and stared at Victor's photo on the computer. Her heart ached in her confusion. She did not really know what her heart was feeling any more. It seemed as though there was a foggy void inside her chest, full of turbulent feelings, but empty at the same time. Melissa was annoyed with herself. She was normally level headed and always in control of her feelings.

Melissa delayed several more minutes, but then shook her head. *I can't delay it any longer*, she said to herself. *I have to call him and tell him that he has to come by the office because I have a new match for him.*

Melissa wanted Victor to come to the office, not for the sake of her job, but for the sake of her emotions. Every time she had seen him, her heart beat as if she was in a race, and the blood in her veins felt as if it were burning.

"Control yourself!" Melissa said aloud. Yet she could not stop the urgent butterflies coursing through her. This was beyond her, and her feelings were unstoppable. Melissa was disturbed by the fact that she was acting in a most uncharacteristic manner.

Melissa picked up the phone and stared at it

for a little before calling the number. A little thrill of excitement ran through her at the thought that she soon would be hearing his voice.

He answered straight away. "Hello." His voice was strong and deep.

Melissa sat there, speechless and thoughtless. It seemed it was an age before she heard her own voice say, "Victor."

"Melissa?"

"Yes." Melissa took a deep breath and launched straight into it. "We have a new match for you for a dinner date. There is a new lady at the agency, and I believe she might be a suitable match."

"Is she Amish?" Victor's voice betrayed traces of amusement.

"No, of course not." Melissa was puzzled. Why would Victor say that? Clearly it amused him, but the joke passed over her head.

"Would you please come by our office to fill in the necessary documents and see if that lady seems suitable for you." Melissa put the phone aside for a second and took a deep sigh.

"I had no idea you were still intending to find another date for me," Victor said.

Melissa was again puzzled. "But that's my job," she said.

There was a long silence. Finally, Victor spoke. "Is she nice?"

"Well, that is something you'll have to decide for yourself. It isn't my business to decide if someone's nice or not. After all, each and every person has their own tastes."

Melissa was going to say more, but Victor cut her off and said, "I'll be there around three," before hanging up the phone without so much as a *goodbye*.

"That was strange," Melissa said aloud. She went to the bathroom, just to look at herself in the mirror. Melissa tried to shrug off the feelings of guilt that washed over her every time she stared at herself in the mirror. No one in the community had mirrors, at least not that she knew. Sure, the *menner* had small mirrors so they could shave, but the women certainly didn't. When she had first come to work at the agency, she had tried to avoid looking in the mirror, and then after a while, had stolen glances from time to time, and now on occasion she would stare at herself for some time.

If I were English, would Victor want to take me on a date? she asked herself, studying her face in the mirror. Melissa suddenly shook herself and hurried from the bathroom. The blood was rushing to her cheeks, and her breath was less than steady. *And for what?* Melissa silently scolded herself. *Just for a phone conversation with a man who is, after all, a client of the company I work for. He's simply a business connection and nothing more.*

Melissa kept telling herself the same words again and again, but to no avail. She was unable to concentrate and was looking at the wall clock every few minutes. To her, a second seemed like ten minutes that would never pass. In fact, that day passed as if it were an entire week. Melissa tried to fill up her time with filing, but was having trouble holding her concentration.

At midday, Milly closed the office door, and the two ate lunch together. "You look quite pale, Melissa," Milly said. "Do you want to take the rest of the day off? I can take over the client for you."

There was no way that Melissa would miss the chance of seeing Victor, so she politely thanked Milly but declined.

After lunch, Melissa managed to gather some energy and concentration, and threw herself back into the filing. She was working as if set on auto mode, just going through the motions and not thinking at all.

At three, there was no sign of the usually punctual Victor, so Melissa had to resist the urge to call him to see if he was indeed coming. After all, she would seem entirely desperate if she did so.

Only a couple minutes later, he appeared at the door, and Melissa left her chair and went to meet him. "Hello, Victor. Please come in."

Victor followed Melissa to the desk, and she showed him some pictures and the social profile of the lady whom she had chosen for the dinner date. Melissa, with mixed feelings, thought the lady looked quite lovely, but it seemed as if Victor was not impressed. "What do you think of her?" she asked.

Victor was silent for a moment. "Do you want me to date this woman?" His eyes were firmly fixed on the screen.

Nee, I want you to date me, Melissa silently screamed. *If only you weren't an Englischer.* Aloud she said, "This is the most suitable match I have found for you."

Victor turned to look at her. "Haven't you overlooked someone?"

Melissa frowned, uneasy under his gaze. "No, I don't think so." *Whatever does he mean?* she wondered.

"All right then, if that's what you want. Where are the forms? I'll fill them in."

It's not what I want at all, Melissa thought. "Just sign this form," she said aloud. "Now, what would be a suitable day and time for you?"

"I don't care. I'll leave it up to you. Just email me whatever day and time suits the lady." With a quick *good bye*, Victor was out the door.

Melissa spoke to the lady's photograph on the computer. "Great, he's left me here to establish the date and time of the date, and then to send both of you the details."

After looking around to make sure that Milly had not overheard her, Melissa sat there, her head in her hands, wondering what was in Victor's mind and what kind of thoughts were laying there. He was so hard to read, and sometimes, he made no sense.

CHAPTER 9

Victor Byler stood at the door of the bishop's *haus*. It was a place he had stood many times before, but still with no resolution.

The bishop opened the door at once and showed Victor into the *haus*. Victor sat down in the adirondack chair, as he had many times before, with the bishop opposite him. Victor thought the adirondack chair a little unusual for indoor furniture, despite the fact that it was covered with a deeply upholstered seat.

The chair was low to the ground, and he felt like a naughty school boy with the bishop, who was sitting in an imposing, four poster, high back, swivel glider, looming over him.

No sooner was he seated, than the bishop's wife set down a tray on the little, round table between them. On it were two cups of hot meadow tea, and a plate of whoopie pies in several colors.

After their silent prayer, the bishop spoke. "Isaiah, oh sorry, Victor as you like to be called these days, have you come to any conclusions since our last conversation?"

Victor shook his head. "*Nee.*" Before the bishop could respond, he added, "Well, sort of."

The bishop simply waved him on.

"As you know, I want a *familye*, and I thought I could have a *familye* with an *Englischer*, but now I realize that's just not possible."

The bishop smiled with a knowing expression on his face, and Victor realized that the bishop had known this all along.

"For so long I've been trying to find a woman I could really love," Victor continued, "a woman who could understand me just the way I am, without the need for any lies or any kind of acting within a relationship. I wanted something natural, something pure, but it's proven to be impossible."

"Do you feel there is an emptiness inside your soul?" the bishop asked.

Victor nodded. "In the beginning, like any young Amish *mann*, I wanted to belong in a relationship. Yet I knew that the woman whom my parents were trying to force me to marry..."Victor hesitated, and looked at his feet. "Well, I felt like something wasn't quite right. In the beginning, I just thought it was me; that I was young and would come to my senses. I began to wonder if there was something wrong with me, but then I thought that surely *Gott* would not want me to enter a loveless marriage?"

He looked at the bishop, but the bishop remained silent.

"I just wanted a happy marriage and a happy *familye*," Victor continued, "I just wanted to be in love. I didn't want anything out of the ordinary; I just wanted to be in love with the woman whom I would marry. My parents said I was selfish." Victor sighed deeply.

"There's a time for everything," the bishop said. "A time for laughter, a time for sorrow, a time for marriage, a time for *kinner*. Do you remember what *Ecclesiastes,* chapter three, says about seasons?" Without waiting for Victor to answer, the bishop quoted -

"For everything there is a
season, and a time for every
matter under heaven -

a time to be born, and a time
　　to die;
a time to plant, and a time to
　　pluck up what is planted;
a time to kill, and a time to
　　heal;
a time to break down, and a
　　time to build up;
a time to weep, and a time to
　　laugh;
a time to mourn, and a time to
　　dance;
a time to cast away stones, and
　　a time to gather stones
　　together;
a time to embrace, and a time
　　to refrain from embracing;
a time to seek, and a time to
　　lose;
a time to keep, and a time to
　　cast away;
a time to tear, and a time
　　to sew;

a time to keep silence, and a
time to speak;
a time to love, and a time to
hate;
a time for war, and a time for
peace."

Victor sat still, contemplating the Scripture.
He wondered how it pertained to his
situation. "Do you mean that *Gott* has
appointed a time for everything? That every
step in life has its proper time - love,
marriage, *kinner*, and so forth? I must admit
I'm behind with those steps, yet I couldn't
marry someone simply because my parents
wanted me to marry her, when I had no
feelings for her whatsoever."

The bishop nodded slowly. "Yet you wanted a
fraa and *kinner*, because you approached the
matchmaking agency."

Victor nodded. "*Jah*, I thought that if I asked

the help of a professional company, maybe, maybe, I would finally succeed in finding the right lady."

"And that did not work." The bishop said it as a statement of fact rather than a question.

Victor shook his head. "*Nee*. I'm going to leave the agency. I asked for *gut*, Christian women, but they did not all have Christian values. Rather, some thought of *Christian* as simply a religion rather than as a personal experience with *Gott*."

"And what about the ladies who did have Christian values?"

Victor looked up at the bishop. "Yes, those were nice, respectable ladies, but I didn't feel truly attracted to any one of them. Something was always missing. I began to wonder if *Gott* meant me to live my life alone."

The bishop nodded and waited for Victor to

go on. "It was frustrating, and sometimes I even got mad at *Gott*."

The bishop raised his eyebrows at that. "So, you have left the agency now?"

Victor nodded. "I had my last dinner date with a match from the agency the other night."

The bishop frowned. "You have only just now, in the last few days, decided to leave the agency?"

Victor was uncomfortable. He did not know how much he should tell the bishop. The bishop, although he had a stern appearance, had always been gentle and understanding with him. Yet Victor was not Amish any more, and he did not know if he should tell the bishop absolutely everything that was on his heart.

"I decided before I went on the dinner date."

"Why did you go on the date then, if you had decided to leave the agency before that?"

A reasonable question, Victor thought, *but one I'm not wholly comfortable answering*. He simply shrugged.

"Tell me about the dinner date." The bishop took a sip of his tea.

Victor shrugged. "It was the same old thing, the same old conversation I've had so many times by now that I could recite it by heart. What about your parents, school, hobbies, education and so on and so forth, but..."

"Go on." The bishop's tone was insistent.

Victor grimaced. "Well, I finally realized that I'm still really Amish. It won't work with an *Englisch* woman." Victor looked at the bishop, and realized that the bishop already knew.

"Have you given more thought about returning to the community?"

Victor nodded solemnly. "Yes, I have given it a lot of thought."

The bishop nodded too. "Then you need to contact Nancy Esh."

CHAPTER 10

Melissa sighed and sank down into her chair. Thank goodness the working day was over. Harriet had called at midday and had told Melissa she was doing a good job, but Melissa herself felt as though she wasn't. Who was she, a Plain girl, to handle the dating issues of *Englischers*? At least she had spent a pleasant afternoon with her beloved filing, and, despite the fact that Milly had to leave early that day, Melissa had not come face to face with any disgruntled *Englischers* who were dissatisfied with their dates.

Melissa was in the front room and about to lock the front door of the agency, when a man burst through the door. He looked annoyed. "Is Harriet Blackwell back yet?" he asked in an urgent tone.

"No, she's not." It took Melissa a moment to recognize the man. "Oh, Mr. Pollard, isn't it?

The man looked Melissa up and down. "Yes, Anthony Pollard. You're the Amish girl who interviewed me, aren't you?"

"Yes, Melissa Glick."

"Oh yes. I'm sorry that I didn't recognize you. I didn't know how many Amish women are working here and you all look alike."

Melissa gasped at the man's rudeness, but he continued. "I didn't mean that the way it sounded. I was in the area, and I just called in to see if you'd found me any suitable dates yet."

Melissa was concerned. She had not found any

suitable dates for Anthony Pollard as he was
new to the agency, and Harriet had not had
time to screen him properly before she had
been called overseas. Harriet had, however,
sent him on one date, but Anthony had
complained that the lady was too old for him.

"Mr. Pollard, I'll make an appointment for you
now. Just let me turn the computer back on. I
was about to lock the office," Melissa added
pointedly.

Melissa made to move around Anthony
Pollard to her desk but he blocked her way,
jutting out his chin in a belligerent manner. "I
don't want to waste any more time. Can't you
find me a date right now?"

Melissa shook her head, worried at the man's
insistence. If only Milly were here. "No, I'm
sorry, Mr. Pollard," she said in the most
decisive tone she could muster. "It's already
after business hours. I'll make an appointment
for you. I'm sure we can help you."

"Why can't you do it now?" Anthony Pollard's tone was petulant, and his face was progressively turning redder. Even his ears were now bright crimson. Gone was the charming smile that Melissa had previously found attractive. Why she'd ever thought him a nice person, Melissa did not know. Now she was faced with an angry English man and she had no idea what to do. She wiped her sweaty hands on her over-apron. This situation was getting out of control.

Anthony Pollard took a step closer to her, looming over her. Melissa automatically took a step back but was unable to move more than a few inches, as the front desk was directly behind her.

"What about you?" he demanded.

"Me?" Melissa heard her voice come out as a squeak.

"I've asked you once before, but you didn't tell me. Do you have a boyfriend?"

Melissa took a quick breath, and tried to force herself to stay calm. "We are not allowed to discuss our personal life with clients," she said slowly and clearly, pleased at least that she sounded somewhat confident this time.

Anthony Pollard screwed up his face in a temper. His now bulging eyes were so close to hers that Melissa could see they were bloodshot. "Just dinner!" he all but yelled. "I just want you to go to dinner with me. What's a little dinner going to hurt?"

Melissa grasped at her throat, fighting the rising panic.

"What's going on here?" The loud, booming voice caused Anthony Pollard to spin around, and when he moved aside, Melissa saw with great relief that Victor Byler was standing in the doorway.

"Nothing." Anthony Pollard spat the word rudely. "I quit this agency. They're useless."

With that, he pushed past Victor Byler and hurried out the door.

Melissa sat on the desk, trembling.

"Are you all right?" Victor at once crossed to her. Melissa found his proximity disturbing, but not at all in the way that she had found Anthony Pollard's proximity disturbing. "You're as white as a sheet," he said, peering at her.

Melissa was afraid she'd cry, and to her dismay, her hands were trembling. "I'll make you some hot tea with sugar," he said, and then hurried to the office kitchen.

That's what people from my community always do when someone's upset, Melissa thought, forgetting her emotional reaction to the unsavory behavior of Anthony Pollard for the moment.

Victor returned and insisted that Melissa sit down. "Here, drink this."

After a few sips of the sugary drink, Melissa did indeed feel a little better. "I hope he doesn't come back to the agency," she said. "He was so rude." Before Victor could respond, Melissa continued. "What are you doing here, Victor? You're not here to complain about your last date, are you?" Melissa was secretly hoping that Victor was, in fact, there to complain about his latest date. Even the thought of it made her feel unreasonably jealous.

"No, it was your horse."

"My horse?"

Victor smiled. "Yes, Blessing turned up at my store just then. You can imagine everyone's shock." Victor chuckled. "Anyway, I brought him back and tied him up very well, and then came up here to tell you."

"How awfully strange. I always make sure he's hitched well, but my brother and his wife have mentioned that he can open gates. This is the first time that he's done anything like this, though, as far as I know."

"Well, thank goodness he did," Victor said, "as if I hadn't come here when I did, you would have had to deal with that unpleasant client."

Melissa clutched at her throat. Yes, whatever would have happened if Victor had not shown up when he did? She did not want to think about it.

"When you've finished your tea, I'll walk you to your buggy." Victor smiled at her.

Melissa liked the way that his eyes crinkled at the corners when he smiled, but then she brought herself up short. *He's an Englischer. No good can come of it, so stop thinking that way*, she silently scolded herself.

CHAPTER 11

As Melissa approached Blessing, she turned to Victor. "I see he's still tied to the rail. And look at the innocent expression on his face," she added, as Blessing turned to her and whinnied softly.

Victor chuckled. "You might have to get some sort of clip and chain to clip between his headstall and the rail, if he can undo ropes."

"*Denki*, that's a *gut* idea." Melissa realized she had lapsed into Pennsylvania Dutch again, but Victor simply nodded.

Melissa reached up to stroke Blessing's neck.

"Why, you're still trembling." Victor's voice was full of concern.

"It's probably as I didn't have time to eat lunch today, and I'm just a little light headed." Melissa hoped she sounded convincing. Her words were true, but she doubted that was the whole reason why she was shaking.

"I'll drive you home," Victor said.

Melissa gasped. "You? But, you can drive a buggy? And how will you get back?" Melissa had forgotten for a moment that Victor was said to be a former Amish *mann*.

Victor took his cell phone out of his pocket and waved it at her. "I'll call a taxi. It's no problem at all."

Melissa shook her head. "Oh no, really. I'll be fine."

"I insist."

Melissa looked at Victor. It was that clear his mind was made up, and she did feel quite shaken after her encounter with the unsavory Anthony Pollard. Besides, she would have the opportunity to spend time with Victor, and despite the fact he was an *Englischer*, she wanted nothing more.

Victor took up the reins and guided Blessing onto the road. Melissa watched him carefully. He was clearly an experienced buggy driver. Could her *aenti's haus* guest, Raymond, be right? Was it true that Victor Byler had once been Amish?

Melissa was somewhat unnerved by the ensuing silence, so said the first thing that came into her head. "How was your date with Linda?"

Victor turned to her and gave her a long, searching look. "Linda is a nice lady, but it won't work between us."

Melissa's heart soared with relief, but she tried

to look business-like. "Oh. I'm sorry to hear that." Her tone was measured.

"You are?" Victor flashed her another look.

What did he mean by that? Melissa wondered. Aloud, she said, "Perhaps it's better if you wait until Harriet returns. She can find you another match." There was no way that Melissa could send Victor on yet another date with another woman; the very thought made her too sad.

"Oh, next turn left," Melissa said, suddenly realizing where they were.

Victor turned Blessing down a winding lane. "I'm leaving the agency."

"You are?" The words were out before Melissa could stop them. She hoped that her pleasure was not too obvious. She should instead be disappointed. After all, the agency was losing a client.

"I've realized that I don't want someone to matchmake me any more."

"You don't?" Melissa asked, and then rebuked herself for sounding so silly.

"*Nee,* I don't."

Melissa jumped in her seat. "Did you just say, '*Nee?*' Did you just speak Pennsylvania Dutch?"

Victor squirmed in his seat, and did not answer. Melissa also remained silent. Finally, Victor said, "I have an Amish man newly working for me."

Melissa bit her lip. *He's avoiding the question,* she thought. Melissa thought things over for a minute. *I might as well come straight out and ask him.* Turning to Victor, she said, "Kannscht du Pennsilfaanisch Deitsch schwetzer?" *Do you speak Pennsylvania Dutch?*

Victor was silent for a moment, and then said, "*Jah,*" before sighing loudly. He added, "I owe you an explanation."

"*Nee, nee,* you don't," Melissa said, embarrassed. "I shouldn't have asked.

Everyone says I'm too forthright, only I'm not forthright enough with Harriet's clients. It's hard to find a middle road." Melissa stopped talking for a moment, doubly embarrassed she was letting her words run away with her. "It's just that the Amish *mann* working for you, Raymond, is staying with my *aenti* and *onkel*, and he said that the *mann* he works for used to be Amish. I shouldn't have said anything."

The buggy was now winding its way down one of the little lanes that traversed the rolling hills on the way to the Glicks' farm. The spring air was cooling with the approach of evening. Despite the awkward situation, Melissa was enjoying the buggy ride with Victor. *If only he was Amish now and taking me on a buggy ride as a courting couple*, she thought, and her heart beat a little faster.

"I *was* Amish, once." Victor blurted out. "I grew up Amish. I had no intention of leaving. I didn't even go on *rumspringa*, and I was going to be baptized, but then I did something that

I was ashamed of, and I left the community. I started my trade as an apprentice cabinetmaker working for an *Englischer*, and then eventually came here and started my own business."

Melissa was shocked by his words. Whatever had he done? It must have been something bad, something dreadful. Sure, it is *Gott* who judges, but Melissa was taken aback by his words. It must have been something terrible to make him leave the community.

"I can see you're horrified." Victor sounded sad.

"It's all just a shock," Melissa said truthfully. Now she could see why Victor had issues. Despite the fact he had left the Amish, he clearly still had Amish values, and not many *Englisch* women shared those. No wonder the agency had not been able to matchmake him successfully.

He needs a woman just like me, Melissa thought.

I would be the ideal *fraa* for him. The thought made her sad. Victor did indeed seem the ideal man, but he had made his choice - he was now English. It was an impossible situation.

Melissa hoped that her parents would be inside the *haus* when she arrived so that they would not see her being driven home by an *Englischer*, of all things. That would prompt too many explanations, but alas, her fears were realized. Both her *mudder* and her *vadder* were standing outside, looking at the vegetable garden, and Victor drove the buggy up to them.

CHAPTER 12

Melissa jumped out of the buggy. "*Daed*, *Mamm*, this is Victor Byler. He's the *mann* that Raymond works for." She hoped her parents would make the connection. "He works near the agency's office and he brought me home as I wasn't feeling well."

"Are you all right?" Her *mudder's* face was full of concern.

"*Jah*, I'll tell you all about it later." To Melissa's relief, her *mudder* nodded, seemingly realizing that there was more to the story, and that Melissa was not comfortable to discuss it with all present.

"Thank you for looking after Melissa," Mr. Glick said. "Did you manage to drive the horse okay?"

Melissa winced. Her *vadder* clearly had not put two and two together. "Mr. Byler used to be Amish," she said. "Remember that Raymond told us?"

Mr. Glick stroked his baard. "*Jah, jah*, I think so."

"Please call me Victor." With that, Victor got down from the buggy. "I'll just call a taxi."

Mr. Glick was still looking thoughtful. "Raymond said that our bishop arranged the job for him and for him to stay with our *familye* members in this community."

Victor nodded.

"So that means you are on familiar terms with our bishop?"

"Matthew!" Mrs. Glick was clearly horrified at her husband's probing remarks.

Victor smiled. "Ich hab nix dagege." *I don't object.* "*Jah*, at times I have talks with the bishop," he added.

Melissa's stomach did cartwheels. Could that mean that Victor was considering returning to the Amish? Why else would he talk to the bishop? Or was it simply as he was talking over his past bad deeds that caused him to leave his community?

"You must stay for dinner." Mrs. Glick's tone was firm.

"Yes, you must." Mr. Glick's tone was equally resolute.

Melissa held her breath. This was too good to be true; a whole dinner spent with Victor, what could be lovelier? Plus her parents might get more information from him over dinner. Would Victor refuse? She held her breath and waited for his reply.

"*Denki*, that would be *gut*."

Melissa let out the breath she had been holding.

Her *vadder* clamped his hand on Victor's shoulder. "Come, we will attend to the horse."

Melissa looked back at Victor and her *vadder* leading Blessing to the barn. She knew that her *vadder* would extract information from Victor, but she knew just as well that she would not be party to that particular information. Melissa wondered why her parents had invited Victor to dinner. She knew that the fact that their bishop knew him would have cleared away any doubts as to his character, but that did not explain why they had actually invited him. Was it because they suspected that he might be interested in courting her? Surely not. He was still an

Englischer after all, and had not given any indication he intended to return to the community.

Melissa could not simply ask her *mudder* as that would show a lack of respect, yet when they were alone in the kitchen, Melissa told her *mudder* all about the incident with Anthony Pollard.

Mrs. Glick gasped, and her hands flew to her cheeks. "Melissa, you must stop working there right now. You must give your notice, *jah?*"

Melissa had been worried that her *mudder* would react in that way. "*Mamm*, I can't let down my boss. She'll be back soon, but until then, I'll make sure I'm never at the office alone."

Mrs. Glick turned back to mashing potatoes. "I'll think about it, but I'm not happy with you working there any more."

Melissa nodded. In fact, she no longer enjoyed

her work there. The filing had been enjoyable, but dealing with the difficult clients who were *Englisch menner* was something else. Even though she would be back to filing when Harriet returned, the incident with Anthony Pollard had soured her time at the agency. Melissa thought that she might in fact hand in her notice when Harriet returned.

Her *mudder's* voice interrupted her thoughts. "Melissa, we were going to have Pot Pie, but now we have a guest, would you get the plate of sliced, roast beef and the plate of roast chicken pieces from the refrigerator, please?"

Soon Melissa and her *mudder* had the table laid with a plate of roast chicken pieces, a heaped plate of roast beef slices, bread that her *mudder* had baked that day, two large bowls of salad and three types of salad dressing, noodles, and a huge bowl of creamy, mashed potatoes, as well as the big pot containing Pennsylvania Dutch Pot Pie, also known as *Bott Boi*.

Before long, Mr. Glick and Victor came in the door. Melissa was suddenly shy. After the silent prayer, everyone tucked in, and there was no conversation for the first few minutes.

Finally, Victor spoke. "It's so *gut* to have Pot Pie again after all these years. It doesn't have carrots in it, does it?"

"*Nee*," Mrs. Glick said. "Many people do add carrots to Pot Pie, but my *grossmammi* and her *grossmammi* before her, never did. I use their recipe - parsley, celery, ham, chicken and beef, with potatoes and square-cut egg noodles. I'm always making those noodles. Oh, and onion."

"It reminds me of my childhood," Victor said. He looked forlorn, and Melissa's heart went out to him.

There was another prolonged silence, and Melissa figured it was because her parents did not wish to ask Victor questions, and so that did not leave much room for conversation.

"Talking of my childhood," Victor said, breaking the silence, "that palomino buggy horse of Melissa's looks exactly like a horse I had when I was a child."

Mr. Glick stroked his *baard*. "I doubt it would be the same horse," he said. "Blessing is only about eight years old."

Victor nodded. "*Jah*, I know it's not the same horse. It's just that the likeness is amazing." Before anyone could speak, he pressed on. "I miss horses. In fact, I miss living on a farm."

"Do you live in an apartment?" Mr. Glick asked.

Victor screwed up his face and nodded. "I live in an apartment over my business. It doesn't suit me at all. I'm not a downtown type of person. I'd like to live on a farm again, with horses and chickens. I also want a dog, but I can't have a dog while living in an apartment and working long hours."

When Melissa lay in bed that night, she could scarcely remember details of the dinner, except that Victor was reminiscing about his Amish childhood. Her *mudder* had not asked any probing questions at all, but Melissa knew that her *mudder* would get all those details out of Mr. Glick that night. After all, her *vadder* and Victor had been away outside for a long time, far longer than it would take to unharness Blessing and see to him.

Melissa let out a long sigh, and then turned over again. Sleep was eluding her.

CHAPTER 13

Melissa adjusted her bonnet and smoothed down her apron, thinking with a smile that any other woman who would be having dinner with Brian Adams would be putting on make up, an elegant outfit, and no doubt six inch, black stiletto heels. Melissa chuckled to herself at the thought. In contrast, her sturdy, black boots made a heavy, knocking sound as she walked down the steps of her *haus*. Outside, the cool evening air made wisps of her dark hair escape from her bonnet and flutter in the wind as she waited for the taxi.

Seated in the taxi, Melissa sent up a silent prayer to *Gott* to ask Him to help calm her bubbling nerves as she made her way to her destination. It was now four weeks since her boss, Harriet Blackwell, had left in a hurry for Barcelona, and she still had not gotten a grip on her new workload.

Dealing with the agency's most difficult, and, needless to say, most demanding, clients was not something for which Melissa was cut out. It made her appreciate her hard working boss more than ever. Now, as she was driven downtown to meet Brian Adams, one of the agency's most difficult clients, *Gott* was the only One who could put her mind at ease.

Melissa knew exactly what she had to do, go in and find out exactly why Brian had not found a single, suitable match after two years as a client with the company. Melissa remembered that Milly had told her that Brian was a typical 'ageist.' Melissa had said, "I know his type to the T. There are a few clients just like him in the company. You know them – the older guy looking for a younger woman to show off as a new trophy to his work buddies."

Melissa did not, in fact, *know them*, but one thing she did know was that she was not impressed by Brian's type. She knew that she was in for a long night as she turned into the restaurant to meet him.

Despite her time working and training with Harriet, Melissa was far from an expert on match making. Filing? That was another matter. She considered herself competent at that, but as for dealing with people face to face, that was indeed another matter entirely. Harriet, on the other hand, always said that she absolutely loved her job and was thrilled when her clients found true love. Harriet knew exactly how to figure out what her clients wanted and what to look for in potential matches.

Harriet always said that some clients made it

easy. They weren't too fussy, but simply just wanted to find love, while others wanted an unrealistic combination of a *Victoria's Secret* model, Martha Stewart, and a stripper named *Honey*, all sealed and delivered with a Masters Degree. Those were the clients for whom Harriet said that she prayed for at church every Sunday.

Melissa sighed. If only they realized that true love was a *Gott*-ordained, spiritual connection between two people, and not something that could be manufactured.

As Melissa made her way toward the entrance of the restaurant, she was crystal clear about her mission, and that was to find out why Brian was stuck with so many unsuccessful matches. She was also there to lay out all his issues on the table. The task itself seemed simple enough, but the latter she found somewhat difficult. While Harriet found it easy to be bold, outspoken, and upfront with her most difficult clients, Melissa was somewhat uncomfortable dealing with *Englischers*, especially ones to whom she should be speaking about issues. Telling *Englischer menner* that they had issues was a daunting prospect. How could she possibly be brutally honest?

"Good evening, Miss Glick, table for two tonight?" Melissa was at first taken aback that the restaurant hostess knew her by name. After all, she had only been there once, but it was the same restaurant that the agency had all their business dinners. Harriet always took her clients there and now it was the 'go to' restaurant for client dining. The staff and chefs knew the *Marriage Minded Agency* team by name and even had a special *Marriage Minded Agency* discount for staff when they dined with their clients.

Despite feeling like a fish out of water in such glamorous surroundings, Melissa had felt comfortable here throughout her dinner with Victor Byler, so hoped the same would be the case that night. The staff had been friendly and the familiar black and red modern décor, the very same colors as the *Marriage Minded Agency's* offices, helped to put her nervous energy somewhat at ease.

"Yes, thank you," Melissa said, as she followed the waitress to her reserved seat in the corner. She fidgeted nervously with her bonnet and adjusted her apron before she sat down to read the menu.

After a while, she looked at the fancy gold clock on the wall. Brian was already ten minutes late. No surprise there. Milly had told her that as the Chairman and CEO of a successful electronic company, Brian was used to having people wait on him. From his company staff, housekeepers, and drivers, Brian had been the man in charge ever since he inherited the multi-million dollar company from his father several years earlier. Milly had warned her that Brian Adams rarely apologized for his tardiness, and ran his company like a drill sergeant.

So far Melissa was highly unimpressed by Brian Adams. Their one meeting had not left her with a *gut* impression of the *mann*. The very thought of him made her edgy and uncomfortable. It was the exact opposite of how she had felt at her last business dinner with Victor Byler. It had been two weeks since her meeting with Victor, and she had not been able to get him out of her head. Her time with him was the most relaxed she had ever been with any of her clients, not that she'd had many clients. He was charming, respectable, and had a good sense of humor. Their conversation had been easy and pleasant.

If only Victor was Amish, Melissa thought with a sigh. He had all the qualities she looked for in a *mann*, not to mention his chiseled, boyish good looks, wavy brown hair, golden flecked, hazel eyes, and that dazzling smile. It left a sting in her heart to know that she was there to help him find love with someone else.

But tonight was not about reminiscing over Victor. Tonight was about Brian Adams, and as he finally made his way toward her, she braced herself.

CHAPTER 14

Brian was taller and bigger than she had remembered. His six foot frame towered above the table. His graying hair was neatly slicked back, showcasing his receding hair line. He was decked out in an impeccably pressed black suit and tie, as if he had just arrived from some exquisite function.

"I'll have a glass of champagne, please. *Cristal*, obviously, but any vintage will do, I'm not a snob," he said with a laugh, before the waitress even had a chance to place his menu on the table. "Are you ready to order?" he asked Melissa with a slight sense of urgency.

Melissa was irritated by his rudeness. After all, he had not even said *Hello*. What's more, she had barely had a chance to look over her menu. Thoughts of Victor had occupied her mind right up until Brian arrived.

Before Melissa was able to make a selection from the menu, Brian jumped in again. "Hey, it's fine. I know the chef. I can have him whip up something." He turned to the waitress. "Sweetheart, tell Paul we would like the steak, medium rare with a side of potatoes. I know it's not on the menu tonight, but tell him it's for Brian Adams."

Melissa could see that the waitress was taken aback by Brian's abrasive instructions, and no doubt, by the fact that he was so rude as to address her as 'Sweetheart'. Melissa found

Brian's pompous show of prestige and wealth particularly disturbing. She was not the least bit impressed by his pretentious display, and it left a sour taste in her mouth.

The waitress collected their menus and raised an eyebrow at Melissa before walking away. Melissa easily interpreted the discreet gesture to mean, *Good luck with this one!* Melissa exhaled deeply.

"So, it's Melissa, right?" Brian straightened himself in the chair as the waitress walked away. "Is Harriet still in Barcelona?"

"Well, *um*, yes," Melissa stammered, suddenly feeling at a loss in dealing with such a high powered individual.

"I'll tell you one thing, I could really use a vacation. Those low lifes on the job have me working overtime," he said, cutting Melissa off before she could finish, and letting out a small chuckle to himself.

"What are you drinking?" he asked suddenly. "Actually, I thought I needed a glass of champagne to help me relax, but if you're anything like Harriet and about to lecture me, I'll need something stronger." He waved to the waitress who was just returning. "A martini, please," he called.

Brian leaned back in his chair and looked at Melissa. "So Melissa, what are you drinking? Oh, you people don't drink, do you? Never mind, I'll order you another glass of water when the waitress comes back around. Now, what new broads do you have in line for me? I must say I haven't been impressed so far."

Melissa almost choked on her water. *Did he just refer to our ladies as 'broads'?* she asked herself.

Brian was still talking. "It's like the ones that Harriet picks for me are always missing something. The last girl you set me up with was really hot, just the way I like them. Tall, slim waist, nice butt, and huge, *umm*, pardon me," he said, and then his face flushed red.

Melissa shifted uncomfortably in her seat and fought the urge to run out of the restaurant.

Brian shrugged, and then launched back into talking. "So, in the looks department, she was good, but she wasn't very smart. When I took her around my work buddies, she could hardly hold a conversation." He leaned back in his chair. "I told her to read up on current affairs so she wouldn't make me look like an idiot in front of my colleagues, but that only made her offended for some reason. Women!" he said with a shrug.

Melissa took a long sip of her water and hoped that the food would come soon. She wanted to eat it fast and then leave as soon as possible.

Brian was on a roll. "The one before that was

really cute. She was smart and funny, but wasn't really good around the house. I mean, on one occasion, I invited her to my penthouse for dinner, and then I got called back to the office for a couple hours. When I got home, she'd already left. She hadn't cleaned up after the dinner or cleaned up around the penthouse. She'd just left, not so much as a note. That's when I realized that I just couldn't take it anymore. I just had to break things off with that one." He snorted rudely. "And she had the nerve to say that she'd wanted to break up with me!"

The waitress arrived with their dinner but Melissa by now had absolutely no appetite. Brian's egotistical and opinionated remarks were too much to endure. All she wanted to do now was call a taxi, and head home. Nevertheless, she was paid to do a job, and so she had better do it well. It just was not good enough to sit there and feel sorry for herself.

Melissa took a deep breath and launched

straight into it. "Well, that's precisely why we planned this dinner. We want to try to figure why it hasn't worked out with any of our arranged matches. All the girls we have selected for you are lovely and intelligent. We have tried quite hard to find suitable matches for you."

It was the first time Melissa had been able to get a word in since the dinner had started. She did not want to offend Brian by telling him that he would never find the right match if he continued to be self-absorbed and arrogant, but she would have to be honest with him to some degree.

"Well..." Brian paused to cut a slice of his steak. "Maybe you and your team aren't trying hard enough. Is it really that hard to find a chick who is young, hot, and intelligent and can cook? Come on, Melissa, you guys are the experts here. Look, I'm not getting any younger. I regret not having kids with my ex-wife, so now I'm kind of in a hurry. Just find me the right girl and we will all be happy."

Melissa let out another deep sigh. She had hardly touched her food, and Brian was now on his second martini and had consumed one glass of champagne. Brian was overwhelming, to say the least, and she was beginning to think that he wasn't good enough for any of the girls in the agency. Dinner with him was far worse than she had expected, and the file on him did not do him justice. He was downright arrogant, self centered, and rude.

Unfortunately, she could not bear to let the truth about how she really felt escape her lips. It was one thing to be considered forthright amongst her own community, but being forthright with this *Englischer* was quite another matter. Instead, she took the more polite route.

"Mr. Adams, I am sorry to hear that the girls in our clientele haven't met your expectations." *Especially when you rotate them on whim every couple weeks*, she added silently to herself. "But I assure you that my team and I will head back to the drawing board to compose a list of new potential matches."

Thankfully, Brian seemed assured with Melissa's response. It wasn't a guarantee, but it was something. At this point, Melissa considered that it would be even harder to find a match for Brian after getting to know him. Would it be fair to set up a lovely girl with someone like him?

Still, this was not Melissa's decision. At the end of the day, he was one of the agency's wealthiest clients, and to lose him because suitable matches turned up futile would be a nightmare. Harriet would be livid if she lost him as a client. Melissa had no choice but to attempt to find Brian his perfect woman.

"Good to hear." Brian rose from his seat. "I have an early meeting tomorrow, so I must get going. Thanks for the dinner. I'm looking forward to hearing from you."

Melissa stood and nodded. "Yes, absolutely." She watched Brian exit the restaurant and then sat back down, relieved that she was no longer in his presence.

Milly had warned her, but she had thought Milly had been exaggerating. Milly had said that Brian Adams was one of the, *No girl is good enough for me*, types and one of the, *I'm too rich for my own good*, types.

That's right, Melissa thought. *He is.*

On the drive home, Melissa's mind wandered to Victor. She wished she had spent the night sitting across from his toned arms and piercing, golden-flecked eyes instead of a balding, egotistical business man sloppily devouring his food in front of her. Her dinner with Brian made her realize that there were very few men like Victor out there. Not only was Victor good looking, but he was respectable. He made her laugh, and she felt at ease with him.

But how was she going to deal with having feelings for a client? No good would come of it. He was not Amish. She needed a second opinion. She needed advice, and she needed it now. She needed her best friend, Isabel.

CHAPTER 15

Melissa's talk with Isabel would have to wait until her lunch break. For now, there was only Milly, and there was no way Melissa would confide her feelings to Milly. They had completely separate world views. That was brought home to Melissa even more so when she entered the office that morning.

"I met someone," Milly squealed, unable to contain her excitement. "He's wonderful, successful, smart, and incredibly handsome. I can't wait for you to meet him!"

"Wait, what happened to Travis Stringer? I thought you were dating him?" Melissa was confused. She had given up trying to keep up with Milly's boyfriends a long time ago. It seemed that Milly changed boyfriends every two months. As far as Melissa knew, Milly had been dating Travis, a young, budding lawyer from California. Milly had talked about him for hours on end, day in and day out.

Milly rolled her eyes. "Melissa, keep up! I broke up with him weeks ago. He was getting boring. Besides, he lives in California so we barely saw each other. Harriet was right. Internet dating just doesn't work."

Melissa was puzzled. "But I thought you loved the fact that he lived in California. You said you had a good time when you went to see him and that you enjoyed the time away."

Melissa knew that *Englischers* had a different view on dating than did the Amish. The Amish were looking to marry, but the *Marriage Minded Agency* was also trying to find marriage partners. In that way, the *Marriage Minded Agency's* view was similar to the Amish view of dating, but Milly, while she worked for the agency, had another view entirely. Why, the very thing Milly claimed to like about Travis was now the very reason that she had broken up with him.

"The distance was wearing me out. Long distance relationships clearly don't work for me." Milly waved her hands to proclaim her frustration.

"Okay." Melissa had no idea what to say.

Milly got out of her chair and walked around to sit on the desk. "Look, Melissa, I know this all sounds strange to you. I'll try to explain. I'm an alpha female. I always have the upper hand in relationships. I never keep a guy around for longer than two or three months and I never fall in love. I fell in love once,"

Milly broke off and shuddered, "and I'm not going down that rabbit hole again."

Now Melissa was entirely puzzled. "Rabbit hole?" she asked.

Milly chuckled. "I mean that I had a painful experience, so I won't be repeating it."

Melissa was glad that the *Marriage Minded Agency* did not share Milly's views. Milly was always hopping in and out of relationships, and her relationships were always short and emotionally unattached. Milly was constantly gushing about her latest date at an expensive restaurant, her vacation at a romantic destination, and the gifts that her doting suitors bestowed upon her.

Without a doubt, the two colleagues were polar opposites. Melissa believed that *Gott* had one woman for one *mann*, and dating in the community was always with a view to marriage. Milly's views on *menner* shocked

Melissa, but she was not one to judge. She knew the English had different ways.

Melissa was now more concerned than ever about her feelings for Victor Byler. Had he been Amish, there would have been no confusion whatsoever, but the fact remained that Victor was not in the community. Did Victor have views similar to Milly's? Melissa had no idea. Surely Victor retained his Amish ideals, but then again, he had been living in the English world for quite some time.

CHAPTER 16

Isabel stopped rearranging candles in the Old Candle Store, and took one look at Melissa's face before speaking. "Melissa, *was its letz?*"

"How do you know something's wrong?"

Isabel tapped her finger on the wooden shelving. "Isn't there?" she countered.

"*Jah.* There's a lot on my mind, and I need your help. I was wondering if you were free this weekend to talk?"

"This weekend? Oh sorry, Melissa, I'm

heading down to the farm this weekend to see my *grossdawdi* and *grossmammi*. It's my *grossdawdi's* birthday."

Isabel's grandparents owned a large farm which was nestled amongst the rolling Lancaster hills. Melissa had spent much of her time there as a child. In fact, it was the scene of Melissa's fondest childhood memories. Isabel and Melissa had spent their days swimming in the pond in summer, or skating on it in winter. At night they would curl up by the camp fire while Isabel's *grossdawdi* told them stories of the Old Testament, of three men who walked into the fire and survived, of Daniel in the lions' den, of Moses and the parting of the Red Sea.

"Why don't you come with me?" Isabel said after a long pause. "It's the weekend, so you don't have to work, and I'm sure your *bruder,* Daniel, and his wife, Nettie, can help your *mudder* if she needs it. Besides, I'm sure my *grossdawdi* would like to see you again."

"Are you sure it's okay?" Melissa asked hesitantly.

"Melissa, of course it's okay. I'll call for you at daybreak. I'm so excited! It'll be just like we're *kinner* all over again."

Melissa could not help but laugh. It was typical of Isabel not even to wait for a response. But her friend was absolutely right. She desperately needed a break. She was not working at the *Marriage Minded Agency* that weekend, and after that nightmarish dinner with Brian Adams, she needed to get a few things off her chest. But most importantly, she needed Isabel to help her figure out what was going on with her feelings for Victor.

"*Denki*, I'll come."

"Of course you will." Isabel chuckled. "Now I had better get back to work. You can tell me all about it later."

The drive down to the farm at the weekend

was exactly as Melissa remembered. The cool, crisp air blew gently against her skin. The tall pine trees arched high into the sky along the smooth, lonely roads, and there was the gorgeous view of the peaceful pond as it kissed the horizon.

"We're here!" Isabel pulled her horse to a stop outside to the farm *haus*.

The girls stepped out and inhaled the delightful springtime air. Melissa looked around her in awe. The farm house was just as she remembered - the brown, rustic, two storey home with its creaky deck, surrounded by large oak trees, the peaceful pond, and the sweet chirping sound of the birds as they fluttered through the trees.

Isabel's grandparents reared chickens, pigs, and buggy horses. They had always sent Isabel and Melissa to feed the animals before breakfast.

Melissa felt at ease and immediately relaxed.

It was as if she were home. It had been years since she visited, and she was thankful it was one of the few things in her life that had remained the same.

"Well, if it isn't my two favorite girls," said a pleasant and familiar voice.

"*Dawdi*!" Isabel exclaimed.

Isabel's *grossdawdi* was just as Melissa had remembered. She had not seen him in years, as they were from another community. *Dawdi* Eli was always decked in oversized trousers, while his *baard* was wild and bushy, and his hair poked out in all directions from under his straw hat.

"Did you girls come to help me feed the chickens before dawn tomorrow morning?" he joked, embracing both girls on either side.

Isabel chuckled. "*Dawdi*, we're here for your birthday!"

"Birthday? I'm too old for those things now! I didn't even remember it was my birthday."

The girls laughed with him.

"Of course we'll help you, *Dawdi* Eli," Melissa said.

"Now, girls, I'm heading into town to collect *Mammi* Olive. She's at her quilting bee. Would you girls like me to get you anything?"

"Marshmallows, please!" Isabel exclaimed.

Dawdi Eli let out a roaring laugh. "Oh yes, I should've known."

A couple hours later, Isabel and Melissa were nestled under cozy blankets and huddled in front of a warm fire. By now, they had unpacked their bags and eaten a birthday dinner with Isabel's grandparents. The cool night air was soothing and the light from the full moon created a perfect glow over the still pond, which could be seen through the large windows. The girls relaxed in their soft chairs as they devoured their favorite treat.

"I missed this," Melissa said.

"*Jah*, me too. I can't get enough marshmallows. *Mmm*, I just love church spread, all those marshmallows mixed with peanut butter, yum. Now, Melissa, *Dawdi* and *Mammi* have gone to bed, so no one can hear. Something's on your mind, what is it?" asked Isabel.

Melissa sighed deeply. "Well, I don't know where to start. First off, I had a business dinner with a most horrible *mann* last night."

Isabel laughed. "He must've been terrible, Melissa. I've never heard you speak badly of someone before. I have a feeling this story is going to be interesting."

Melissa just shrugged. "His name is Brian Adams, and he is one of the agency's wealthiest clients. So far, it hasn't worked out with him and any of our matches. It was my job to take him out on a business dinner and try to figure out what his issues are, since Harriet is still in Barcelona. And let me tell you, as soon as he sat down, I wanted to run."

Isabel sat forward in her chair. "Why, what was wrong with him?"

"You mean, what wasn't wrong with him?" Melissa chuckled. "I don't know how to say this politely, Isabel."

"Just say it. You're usually forthright."

"Well, Milly says that he's egotistical, and that he thinks that because he's wealthy and owns his own company, that he thinks that he can withdraw and deposit girls like he's at an ATM."

"And you agree with Milly?"

Melissa nodded. "He wants a young, attractive woman, but he's old and balding. I hope *Gott* forgives me for saying this, but the mere sight of him makes me uncomfortable. In all good conscience, I cannot send anyone on a date with him. And the worst part is, that if I don't find him someone and we lose him as a client, Harriet will be upset with me."

Isabel shifted in her seat. "I'm so sorry you had to deal with that. I know you love your job and it's very important to you, but do you think you should continue on there?"

Melissa hurried to reassure her. "It's only until Harriet gets back, although the events of the last few days have made me wonder whether I do want to stay there at all, even to do the filing." There was a time of silence, and then Melissa added shyly, "Actually, the worst part is, that when I was having that awful dinner with Brian Adams, I couldn't stop thinking about Victor Byler the entire time."

Isabel gasped, and her jaw dropped. "You do like this Victor, don't you! I knew it the moment you told me about him. When you told me about your dinner with Victor, you kept saying how at ease and comfortable you felt with him, how much he made you laugh, and how you melted when he smiled. You never once admitted that you were falling for him, but it was obvious to me."

Melissa covered her face with her hands, and her ears burned with embarrassment. "I couldn't stop thinking about Victor the entire time I was with Brian Adams. Victor is the exact opposite. He is kind, gentle, respectful, and charming. There is just one problem."

"Yes," Isabel said, "and a big problem at that. He's English."

"*Jah*, well, perhaps."

"Perhaps?" Isabel said. "How can someone be *perhaps* an *Englischer*?"

Melissa laughed at the look on Isabel's face. "I don't want to get my hopes up, but he used to be Amish."

For the second time, Isabel leaned forward in her chair. "Go on," she said with interest.

"He had dinner with my *familye*..."

"He what?" Isabel shrieked, and then put her hand over her mouth and looked up the stairs. "I hope I didn't wake up *Dawdi* and *Mammi*."

Melissa wrung her hands. "It's all a bit complicated. Victor was Amish, and then something happened and he left. He still seems Amish though. He spoke in Pennsylvania Dutch all through dinner with my *familye*."

Isabel interrupted Melissa yet again. "How did it happen that he had dinner with your *familye*?"

"I was coming to that. He took me home, and my *mudder* insisted he stay for dinner. Well, he seemed quite keen to stay for dinner. He told us all that he'd been brought up Amish, and that he only left his community a few years ago. He'd told me earlier that he did something he was ashamed of, and he left the community."

"He was shunned?"

"*Nee*, he hadn't been baptized. I think he was quite young. He hasn't told me what it was, and my parents didn't ask him."

Isabel nodded. "Melissa, have you ever considered the fact that Victor might return to the community? Have you thought that maybe he might actually have been considering it? It sounds like you two have a very strong connection. You don't know for sure unless you get to know him better. You might be surprised." Isabel ended with a smile.

Melissa was quiet. "I hope that you're right," she said in a small voice. "I just don't want to get my hopes up."

"You have plenty of hope. Here, pass me

that." Isabel pointed to large books on a little, wooden table next to Melissa.

"What, the *Martyr's Mirror*?"

"*Nee*, the Bible."

Melissa reached over and took the Bible, which she handed to Isabel.

"Where is that Scripture?" Isabel muttered to herself, thumbing through the Bible. "*Ach*, here it is, Romans chapter five, verses two through five." Isabel read aloud -

> Through him we have also
> obtained access by faith into
> this grace in which we stand,
> and we rejoice in hope of
> the glory of God. Not only
> that, but we rejoice in our
> sufferings, knowing that
> suffering produces
> endurance, and endurance
> produces character, and

character produces hope,
and hope does not put us to
shame, because God's love
has been poured into our
hearts through the Holy
Spirit who has been given
to us."

The two sat quietly for a moment and pondered the Scripture. After a while, Isabel spoke. "If it is *Gott's* Will that you marry Victor, it will be so. You have to place your hope on *Gott's* Will."

Melissa nodded, and then yawned widely. "Your advice is always *gut*, Isabel, *denki*."

"Just think about it. Now let's go to bed; remember you promised *Dawdi* that you'll be feeding those chickens tomorrow before first light."

"You'll be feeding them too!" Melissa said with amusement.

"*Nee*, I will be fast asleep," Isabel said, as the girls headed up the stairs. Melissa gave her friend a playful shove. Her talk with Isabel was exactly what she needed. She definitely had a lot of thinking to do.

CHAPTER 17

The following week, Melissa arrived at Isabel's place of work in a breathless state.

Her friend looked up in alarm. "*Was der schinner is letz?*" she asked.

"Nothing's wrong. It's just that Harriet is on her way back and I don't know whether to give notice or not. I wanted to talk it over with you before I come to a decision."

Isabel nodded. "Okay, well it's time for my

lunch break. I'll just tell Mr. Harrison that I'm going."

Isabel disappeared into the back room and reappeared moments later. "Let's go."

The two girls hurried to their favorite café. No sooner than they were seated at their usual table overlooking the street, than the waitress hurried over to take their order. Melissa ordered first. "A sugar and spice latte, and a smoked salmon bagel, please."

The waitress looked at Isabel. "A chai tea latte and a smoked ham, cold sandwich on multigrain, sunflower bread please."

The waitress smiled and left. "You know," Isabel said, "I didn't see her write anything down, did you?"

Melissa chuckled. "*Nee*. She probably just wanted to make sure that were having the same thing that we always have."

The two girls laughed, but suddenly, Melissa grabbed Isabel's hand. "Don't look around."

Isabel at once turned around.

"Isabel! I said not to turn around."

"Sorry. Why, what shouldn't I be looking at?"

"It's Victor Byler."

Isabel's face lit up. "Oh, I really want to see him. Can't I take just a little peek?"

Melissa shook her head. "*Nee, nee*, he's with an Amish woman. They're sitting in the secluded booth right over in the back corner."

Isabel at first looked concerned. "*Hmm*, well I suppose it could be his *mudder*, or his *schweschder*. Don't jump to conclusions."

"He's an only child," Melissa whispered. "I've read his file. And she's too young to be his *mudder*. His back's to me, but I can see her face clearly. She's a young, pretty Amish woman, and their heads are close together."

"Are you sure it's him?" Isabel asked as their drinks arrived. She briefly stole a glance over her shoulder. "You can't really see much as the booth's partially obscured. You can really only see the girl's face."

"*Jah, jah*," Melissa said. "It's him all right. Plus I don't recognize the girl, so she can't be from our community."

"I only got a quick look, but I didn't recognize her either. Melissa, I've said it once and I'll say it again, don't jump to conclusions. She could be anyone."

Yet try as she might, Melissa was unable to do anything other than jump to conclusions. "Isabel, could we please get our lunch to go? I truly can't sit here looking at Victor all the time."

Isabel raised her eyebrows but did as Melissa asked. The two girls took their lunch to a nearby park. Isabel chatted away happily, but

Melissa was unable to concentrate. Who was the Amish girl? And what was she to Victor?

By the time Melissa arrived back at the office, she was in turmoil, and still scolding herself for having feelings for an *Englischer*. He wasn't exactly wholly an *Englischer*, but the fact remained that he was not Amish; he was not back in the community. There was no future with any *mann* who was not in the community. Melissa sighed loudly. Perhaps Victor was intending to come back to the community, and marry the Amish girl? Of course, it was obvious. Why hadn't she realized it before?

Melissa was sure she had figured it out. She had mistaken Victor's interest in returning to the Amish, for interest in her. He had been speaking to the bishop because he intended to return to the community, and now, he had brought his betrothed over to their town, likely to meet the bishop, as he intended to continue to live here when he was married. It all fitted together. How could she have been so stupid?

Melissa sank into the depths of despair, despair over her feelings for Victor, and despair that she had been so silly. Melissa threw herself into the filing, which only somewhat took her mind off her situation. Near the end of the day, the computer froze. It used to freeze all the time, but then several weeks ago had started working again.

Melissa was about to call Milly, when she came into her office. "Oh, Milly, I was just coming to get you. The computer's frozen again."

Milly sighed. "I think Harriet will have to replace it. I thought it was fixed. Here, I'll have a go. Sometimes I can get it to work again. Anyway, we're out of termination forms, and I need to print out a set right now. There's a man at the front desk to see you. One of the difficult clients, he's leaving the agency." She tut-tutted. "Harriet won't be pleased."

Melissa walked out, her heart in her mouth, worried that the client might be Anthony Pollard, only, standing in front of her with a wide smile on his face, was Victor Byler.

"Victor, you're leaving the agency," she blurted.

Victor looked puzzled. "I'd thought I mentioned that before."

Melissa bit her lip. "Oh yes, you did."

Victor took a step toward her. "You're not happy that I'm leaving the agency? I thought you'd be happy."

Melissa was entirely puzzled. Why would she be happy that he was leaving the agency? She'd never see him again. "But, why?" she stammered.

A look of confusion passed across Victor's face. "I thought you'd know."

Melissa shook her head and tried to avoid his gaze. Had Victor seen her at the café after all? If so, then she would be expected to know that he had a girlfriend and so was leaving the agency. *That must be the explanation*, Melissa thought with dismay.

"I've got them!"

Both Melissa and Victor looked up at Milly, who was waving some forms. "The termination forms. I managed to print them," she said as an aside to Melissa.

Melissa took the opportunity to leave the room, but despite her misgivings, could not stop herself listening on the other side of the door.

"We're sorry to see you go, Mr. Byler," Milly said. "Can you tell me why you're leaving?"

Melissa could not hear Victor's response but

then realized that he had not yet answered. "Well, I've fallen in love," he finally said.

"That's wonderful," Milly said. "Is it one of our ladies?"

Melissa turned away. She knew the answer to that one. Victor was getting married to the Amish girl at the café. She had been such a fool.

CHAPTER 18

Milly came back into the room. "Mr. Byler wants to speak to you again."

Melissa shook her head. "Please tell him that I'm not available."

Milly gave her a strange look but disappeared to do as she asked.

Melissa looked at the clock on the wall. Thank goodness, it was time to leave for the day. When Harriet returned, she would give her notice. She walked into the front office, looking around the door first to see if Victor was still there. "Milly, has he gone?"

Milly nodded. "What was all that about?"

Melissa shrugged. "I've had enough of the difficult clients. 'Bye, Milly."

"Goodbye, Melissa. I'm about to close up."

Melissa walked to her buggy, filled with conflicting emotions. When she reached her parking place, she groaned aloud. Could the day get any worse? Blessing was gone. She walked over and looked at the double clip she had used to tie him. The clips seemed to be working well enough, so how had he gotten away? Well, that wasn't the issue; the issue was to find him, and fast.

Melissa looked around, and then it dawned on her. Blessing had gone to Victor Byler's store before. What if he had gone there again? That could prove awkward and embarrassing.

Melissa hurried in the direction of Victor's

store, hoping that one of his staff members would find Blessing and be on their way back with him right now. She sent up a silent prayer as she hurried. *Please help me, Gott.*

When Melissa turned the corner, she saw to her great relief that Blessing was tied next to Raymond's horse and buggy. Melissa let out a long sigh of relief. Someone must have caught him and tied him up, and this time, Blessing had been content to stay put. She hurried over to him. "Blessing, I was so worried."

"That's twice he's turned up here," said a gentle voice.

Melissa swung around to see Victor standing behind Blessing.

"Oh, Victor! Sorry, I didn't see you there."

Victor walked over to her. "Melissa, I'm sorry if I've upset you."

Melissa groaned inwardly. This was rapidly

turning embarrassing. "*Nee, nee*, not at all," she said. "Congratulations."

"Congratulations?" Victor frowned, and scratched his head.

Oh, I've put my foot in it, Melissa thought. *He'll know I found out that he said that he's in love with someone*. Melissa didn't know what to say, so her mouth went into overdrive. "*Err*, yes, you told Melissa you were in love with someone, so I meant congratulations on that, and on returning to the community. Oh well, I figure that you're returning to the Amish, as she's Amish."

"She?" Victor's brows met in the middle.

Why did he say that? Melissa wondered. "Yes, the Amish lady in the café."

"The café?"

"Oh, you didn't know I was there. I was having lunch with my friend, Isabel, and I saw you in the café with the Amish lady."

Victor's face suddenly lit up. "Ahhhh!" he said. "That explains everything. Now I see."

Melissa frowned at him. She was a little cross that he looked so happy when her feelings were so hurt.

"Melissa, can we go for a walk in the park? There are some things I want to explain to you."

Melissa wanted to walk in the park with Victor, just to be close to him, but she did not want to prolong the agony and she did not want to hear him profess his love for the Amish girl. "*Nee*, I'd best be getting back to my *haus*."

"Please, Melissa, it's important."

Melissa stood there in two minds.

"Please." His tone was urgent.

"All right then." *You fool, Melissa*, she thought, silently scolding herself for giving into him.

Melissa followed Victor into the park, and across the well maintained lawns. It was a lovely day, with happy ducks splashing under the fountain, but the beauty of the day was lost on Melissa, just as it had been in her earlier visit to the park that day. Victor turned onto the paved walking path that traversed the length of the park, running alongside the stone waterway.

Finally, just past the large, white gazebo, Victor came to a stop. "Shall we sit here?"

"*Jah*." Melissa just wanted to get it all over with. The colorful flowers were giving off all kinds of pleasant fragrance, and the tinkling of the little waterfall was soothing. Only Melissa was not relaxed, as Victor was about to tell her that he was engaged to another woman.

"The lady you saw me with was Nancy Esh, or rather, she used to be."

Melissa was a little confused by that, but she sat in silence.

"Nancy Esh is the reason why I left the Amish."

Despite herself, Melissa was now intrigued.

"My parents and Nancy's parents had been *gut* friends for years and always joked that the two of us would be married one day. When we turned seventeen, our parents tried to pressure us to marry. Nancy wanted to marry me, but I didn't want to marry Nancy. I wanted to be in love with my *fraa* and I wasn't in love with Nancy. The pressure was so strong, that I left the Amish. I took the coward's way out, and fled."

Melissa turned to look at Victor, taking in his golden-flecked eyes. "You didn't tell Nancy that you didn't want to marry her?"

Victor shook his head. "That's just it. I did tell her, more than once, and she always went into floods of tears. I told my parents again and again that I didn't want to marry Nancy, but they said I was young and foolish. In the end, I just ran away and became English."

Melissa bit the end of one fingernail. "Is that the terrible thing that you did?" Melissa did not think it so terrible at all.

"*Jah*, it was."

"But really," Melissa said. "I can't see what else you could have done. You couldn't marry Nancy if you weren't in love her... then," she added, sad that Victor was now in love with Nancy.

"Anyway, to cut a long story short," Victor continued, "I always felt I had done the wrong thing, and I've been talking to the bishop for some time about returning to the community, although I was in two minds about it at first. The last time I saw him, the bishop said I needed to contact Nancy to ask her forgiveness."

Melissa was puzzled. "Did the bishop think you did the wrong thing? Did the bishop think you should have married Nancy back then?"

Victor shook his head. "*Nee*, it wasn't that. I was the one who thought I had done the wrong thing, so the bishop told me to contact Nancy so that the past could be resolved."

"I see."

"So I wrote to Nancy," Victor continued, "and she agreed that it needed to be resolved, so she came to see me."

Melissa could not help but feel jealous. She sat silently and waited for Victor to continue.

"Nancy said that she had completely forgiven me," Victor continued. "In fact, she had forgiven me some time ago. She and her husband felt they should come and tell me that Nancy had forgiven me, so that I could go forward with my life."

Melissa scratched her ear. What had Victor just said? "Husband?" she said aloud. "Whatever are you talking about?"

"Nancy and her husband, Dan, came to have lunch with me today," Victor said.

Melissa scrunched up her face. "I didn't see any Dan."

"He was sitting next to Nancy."

"Oh!" Melissa realized that she had only a partly obscured view of the booth, and that Dan must have been sitting on the other side of Nancy. "But then why did you tell Melissa that you were leaving the agency, since the Amish woman you're in love with is married?" Melissa looked down at her boots.

Victor chuckled. "I'm not in love with Nancy. I never was, and I'm certainly not now."

"But then why did you tell Melissa that you were in love?" Melissa turned to look at Victor, and then it dawned on her. "Oh." Her cheeks flushed hot. Could he possibly mean what she hoped he meant?

Victor took her hand in his. "Melissa, my love, you're the only woman I've ever been in love with."

Melissa gasped. Everything seemed to slow down. Could this be true? She hoped it wasn't simply a dream.

"I've told your *vadder*..."

"My *vadder*!" she gasped.

Victor nodded. "*Jah*, I have your *vadder's* permission to court you, if you'll have me. The bishop knows too. I'm returning to the community. I'm taking instruction, and I'm going to be baptized."

Melissa could scarcely contain the excitement that was bubbling up within her. She had thought there was no hope, but how wrong had she been. "*Jah, jah*, of course I want to," she said, breathlessly.

Victor put his arm around her, and pulled her close. As their lips met softly, Melissa sent up a silent, heartfelt prayer of thanks to *Gott* who had in fact, done abundantly more than all she had ever hoped.

NEXT BOOK IN THIS SERIES

Charity

Isabel, while working at the Old Candle Store, is the witness to a crime. The handsome detective heading the case left the Amish years ago due to the community's forgiving attitude to a serious crime committed on his brother. Despite the sparks that fly between them, can the two ever be together, when they have opposing views on forgiveness, violence, and punishment?

ABOUT RUTH HARTZLER

USA Today best-selling author, Ruth Hartzler, was a college professor of Biblical history and ancient languages. Now she writes faith-based romances, cozy mysteries, and archeological adventures.

Ruth Hartzler is best known for her Amish romances, which were inspired by her Anabaptist upbringing. When Ruth is not writing, she spends her time walking her dog and baking cakes for her adult children, all of whom have food allergies. Ruth also enjoys correcting grammar on shop signs when nobody is looking.

www.ruthhartzler.com

Made in the USA
Monee, IL
29 August 2021